Sea Change

A Novel by
William Grovère

Sea Change
A Novel

ISBN: 9-798218-994761

To my five grandchildren:
Faith, Logan, Jack, Travis, Avery—
Cedric's contemporaries.

Acknowledgements

With grateful appreciation to Sandrine Ricote for meticulous text editing, my wife, Sylvia, for tireless editing and Tom Waller for valuable feedback.

Special thanks to Gigipaws for the cover painting depicting the French battleship, *Napoleon*—the first ship of the line to use a steam engine in 1850.

Sea Change

A novel by
William Grovère

Table of Contents

Book I 1

Chapter 1: Back Pain 2

Chapter 2: Sea Trial 13

Chapter 3: 70 Knots 22

Chapter 4: Interrogation 31

Chapter 5: The Bastion of Orthodoxy 43

Chapter 6: Café Quai d'Isère 49

Chapter 7: Royalties 55

Chapter 8: The Syndicate 65

Chapter 9: Magnetic Moments 73

Chapter 10: Sofia 82

Chapter 11: Neutronetics 93

Chapter 12: Downhill 104

Chapter 13: The Quad 110

Chapter 14: The Health Spa 117

Book II 123

Chapter 15: Christmas Toys 124

Chapter 16: Dark Clouds 131

Chapter 17: Paris 138

Chapter 18: Career Change 144

Chapter 19: The Polaris Explorer 149

Chapter 20: Dual Use 157

Chapter 21: Extraction 167

Chapter 22: Mugs 178

Chapter 23: Heavy Lift 186

Chapter 24: Skeletons in the Closet 193

Chapter 25: New Start 202
Chapter 26: Timecharging 209
Chapter 27: The Briefing 221
Book III 229
Chapter 28: Bleak Night 230
Chapter 29: Redirection 235
Chapter 30: Extortion 244
Chapter 31: Justice 250
Chapter 32: Requiem 255
Chapter 33: The Mole 261
Epilogue 264

Book I

Chapter 1: Back Pain

Charles stepped out of the elevator on the second floor instinctively looking to the left and right to see if he was alone in the corridor. His destination was at the far end on the right, a brightly lit reception area behind a swinging glass door with the words, "*Centre de Chiropratique Portzic*" neatly stenciled on the door, followed by "*sur rendez-vous uniquement*". Charles entered in his customary fashion.

"*Bonjour, Monsieur Gilbert*," said the receptionist upon his entry. "How is your back feeling today? Captain Rousseau is running late. May I offer you a cup of coffee?"

"*Oui, s'il vous plaît*," said Charles, taking a seat in the waiting room.

The receptionist returned momentarily, handing him a cup of café latté with a biscuit on the side. "Your usual," she said without further comment before returning to her position behind the reception desk.

There was a replica of a famous oil painting on the wall of Le Phare de la Jument lighthouse off the coast of Île d'Ouessant being bashed by towering waves. The painting captured the merciless majesty of the wild North Atlantic off the West Coast of France during a storm. The painting had a way of sucking Charles into a reverie of his memory of a terrifying experience at sea in such a storm. The twenty-minute wait for his host passed unnoticed.

The glass door swung open with Captain Jacques Rousseau briskly entering the office suite. "Oh, Charles! I am so sorry. I got snarled in traffic."

"No problem, Jacques," replied Charles, "I was just taking a fantasy voyage in my sailboat around La Jument—at night—trying to find the harbor entrance. It's a miracle I didn't perish that night."

Capt. Rousseau headed back to his office without stopping. Charles stood and followed, leaving his empty cup on the corner of the reception desk. "How did that adventure end?" Jacques asked without turning around.

"I was pretty reckless in those days. It was before I met Gabrielle," said Charles. "I knew a storm was approaching, but I thought I would make it to the harbor before it got dark. I didn't anticipate that I would be sailing head-on into a gale. I radioed a distress call once I realized I was in real trouble but got no response. The beacon from the lighthouse was blinding but I couldn't see the rocks in the dark. The wind was blowing me towards them, and I had pretty much abandoned all hope when I caught sight of the searchlight from a rescue craft. I lost my sailboat, but those brave souls managed to save my life."

The two men walked down the hallway past a couple of rooms equipped with the kind of machines that chiropractors use to straighten spines. One room sported a full-sized skeleton replica dangling from a pole. It was all for cover. No chiropractors or medical doctors of any sort worked there. They were in a top-secret facility adjacent to the navy base in Brest, on the west Atlantic coast of France, the existence of which was known only to a select handful of people at the highest echelons of the French Intelligence Ministry. They entered a small conference room at the end of the hallway with an oval wood table surrounded by four swivel chairs. The only other feature was a flat panel video screen on the far wall. Jacques pulled the door closed behind them. There were clicks as several dead bolts engaged, and a light over the door turned red, indicating that the SCIF was secure.

They were inside a Sensitive Compartmented Information Facility for a briefing on matters of profound importance to national security.

Jacques switched on the flat panel display. A live webcam view from the top of the Arc de Triomphe facing southwest down the Avenue des Champs-Élysées came on. Low-hanging clouds of early April were producing light drizzle.

While they waited for the remote meeting to begin, Charles asked, "Was it really necessary to completely discredit Cédric Rothschild?"

"We could have sent him to prison," replied Jacques with a chuckle.

"On what charge?"

Jacques leaned back in his swivel chair grinning. "On the charge of knowing too much," he replied.

"That's absurd," shot back Charles. "That's the kind of thing dictatorships do."

"I was only kidding," said Jacques. After pausing for serious effect, "You know that this Rothschild character is a real threat to our national security—not him personally. He is as loyal a Frenchman as it gets. It's just that his theories are destabilizing. We need to keep the discovery of microfusion out of the hands of the Syndicate pirates."

"For how long? We can't keep it secret forever," replied Charles.

"We must keep microfusion secret for however long it takes to eliminate the Syndicate naval threat. I don't need to remind you, Charles, of the impact that microfusion can have on naval power. It will give the French Navy an unprecedented advantage on the high seas."

"Perhaps," replied Charles. "It's just sad that we had to savage the inventor's reputation."

"I would hardly characterize the treatment Cédric is getting at the GRL as 'savage'," said Jacques. "He is being treated like royalty. It has taken longer than expected for the other scientists to warm up to the notion of variable light speed, but fortunately, microfusion works regardless of the theoretical explanation. In time Cédric will get the recognition he deserves. Meanwhile, we don't want to encourage any Syndicate spies to be snooping around Grenoble pumping him for information. Of all people, you should know that Cédric can't stop talking about his theories to anyone that will listen."

The video screen flashed to a slide introducing "Headquarters of the French Intelligence Ministry, Paris" followed by a live shot of a group of people taking their seats around a conference table.

"Good morning, Captain Rousseau. Is your SCIF secure?" came a voice over the intercom from the man seated at the head of the table.

"Good morning, Director. Yes sir, the SCIF is secure," replied Jacques. "I would like to introduce Mr. Charles Gilbert. I have asked him to accompany me on the sea trial tomorrow."

"Yes, Mr. Gilbert. I have heard a lot about you, and it is nice to finally meet you. Please proceed with the briefing, then," said the director.

Jacques started in, "My engineering manager is confident that the frigate is ready for her first sea trial tomorrow. The ship is now out of drydock and a minimum contingent of the crew is on board receiving pre-deployment training. We have managed the repurposing of the frigate while in dry dock to give the appearance of a routine service-life extension. The commander and the executive officer are the only ones onboard that know the true nature of the deployment tomorrow other than my engineers. The ship has been retrofitted with twin 50-megawatt microfusion steam turbine reactors, replacing the original 10-megawatt gas turbines. Additionally, the deck guns have been replaced with electromagnetic rail guns that can fire 30 rounds per minute, but these will not be tested on this sea trial. We have managed the secrecy of the mission up to this point, but by this time tomorrow, you can be sure that rumors will begin to circulate once the crew experiences what the ship can do. With the combined one-hundred megawatts of electric power driving the main propulsion jets, it is estimated that the ship will have a top speed of 80 knots." Jacques paused to allow this last comment to sink in. "You know, Director, this means the power to weight ratio of this ship approaches that of a jet ski. Without the need for missile silos, projectile magazines or fuel tanks, the ship only weighs 2,500 gross tons."

"Why such a large ship, then?" asked the director. "Wouldn't a smaller ship have sufficed?"

Jacques answered, "It turns out that every available cubic centimeter of the hull space is crammed with the supercapacitors needed to fire the rail guns."

"Very good, then," replied the director. "We will eagerly await your assessment when you return to port. As you know, the Syndicate has been stepping up its pirate raids on commercial shipping and there are a lot of people eager to see this vessel go into action to stop them." He looked around the table to see if anyone had further questions. After a short pause, he stared into the camera and said, "Jacques, something has come up that I need to make you aware of. It's the real reason I called for this briefing. Mr. Rothschild was becoming a bit of a nuisance, so he was reassigned to what we believed was a harmless project in the astrophysics division where he would not be able to continue creating discord among the microfusion scientists. What we failed to take into account is that he would use the opportunity afforded to expand his research regarding his theories about antigravity. He is now claiming that, not only is the speed light not constant, but that the universal gravitational constant is not constant either. If true, this is sure to turn the world upside down. Some of the scientists at Grenoble inform me that these theories may not be as far-fetched as they previously thought. I have been told that Charles possesses some kind of levitating magic 'pea' that exhibits some unusual behavior. I am eager to hear more about this."

This last comment caused Charles to cast a puzzled glance across the table at Jacques. "That's all for now," said the director, adding, "I look forward to your report when you return from the sea trial tomorrow."

Just like that, the screen returned to the webcam atop the Arc de Triomphe. Charles leaned back in his chair to process what he had just heard. "How in the world does he know about Cédric's 'pea'?" he asked.

Jacques shrugged his shoulders pretending to look innocent.

"What's this about electromagnetic rail guns?" inquired Charles.

Jacques replied, "You need to forget that you heard that. It's above your security clearance level. By the way, how many hard copies of Cédric's variable light speed manuscript do you think are still out there?"

Charles replied, "There is, of course, the printed copy that Cédric gave me at NaPiles. It is safely tucked away in my personal safe at home."

"You should have surrendered it when the French authorities took over your facility," Jacques said. "You are in possession of an unauthorized classified document. I think that comes with some jail time," he added jokingly.

Charles made no comment and continued the inventory without addressing further the existence of his personal manuscript copy. "Knowing Cédric as I do, it is unlikely that he kept multiple copies laying around his apartment. My guess is that he kept an electronic copy only on his computer."

"Yes. We obtained that one when we confiscated it."

"You did what?" shot back Charles shaking his head in dismay. "Really, Jacques, did you also confiscate his driver's license and passport?"

"Of course," replied Jacques. "He is a flight risk, you know."

"But he's not a criminal!" protested Charles, shaking his head in bewilderment.

Jacques countered, "We returned his computer as soon as it was 'sanitized'. Charles, microfusion is the most disruptive technology for maritime propulsion ever..."

"No. I beg to differ," Charles interrupted. "That would certainly be nuclear propulsion. I served on a French nuclear submarine, so I should know."

"No, Charles. I disagree. Nuclear propulsion technology can only be practiced by rich and powerful nations that can afford it. There aren't many of those left these days. What really makes microfusion so disruptive is that it can be practiced by anyone with a garage shop. You proved this at NaPiles. Once you and Cédric figured out how to fabricate neutron clusters, the rest was rather easy."

"Except it took a brilliant mind like Cédric's to explain how it works based on his theory that the speed of light was six orders of magnitude slower inside the neutron cluster," said Charles.

"It was not actually necessary to explain how it works," replied Jacques. "You and Cédric demonstrated that deuteron fusion takes place in neutron clusters. The theory behind it doesn't matter. Most of the scientists in Grenoble remain dubious that the phenomenon needs to be explained by the speed of light being affected by the local mass."

"At some point they will have to accept Cédric's ideas," said Charles.

"Reluctantly," replied Jacques. "That's all the more reason to keep microfusion under a cloak of secrecy. We can't run the risk of having Cédric's theories leaking out. If antigravity is another consequence, as the director just suggested, then it is even more urgent that none of Cédric's manuscripts remain out there."

Charles continued, "As far as I know Cédric was ostracized and had no scientific colleagues with whom to discuss his ideas. There is the possibility—likelihood, rather—that copies remain with the reviewers for the journal he submitted the manuscript to while he was a graduate student at Candlebridge. Since the manuscript was rejected, there's no way to know. It may be worth seeing if the journal is willing to disclose the names of the reviewers, but that is unlikely. His thesis advisor may also have kept a copy."

"Something else I should probably make you aware of, Charles. We assigned a female scientist from our intelligence division to keep tabs on Cédric and to distract him. Apparently, the scheme is working because the two have become romantically involved to some degree."

"A seductress spy?" exclaimed Charles.

"Magdalena is no seductress, Charles. We needed to insert someone that was Cédric's intellectual equal. There is probably no such person on this planet, but she is extremely bright and charming nonetheless."

"So, you planted a spy to watch over Cédric?" repeated Charles.

Jacques replied, "In a word, yes. But she is a brilliant mathematician. Mathematics is not one of Cédric's strong suits, so the pairing was rather clever on my part, don't you think?"

"Oh, Jacques. What have you dragged me into?" exclaimed Charles rhetorically.

Jacques stood up and disengaged the locks, extinguishing the red light over the door. "What do you think of your room at the Officer's Club? I tried to book the VIP suite but had to settle for ordinary officer's quarters. I hope that's okay. I suggest we have an early dinner at the club dining room and turn in for the night. The frigate sails at 0500 hours, so we need to depart the Officer's Club no later than 0430."

Chapter 2: Sea Trial

The frigate slipped quietly in the dark past Le Phare du Petit Minou lighthouse on the north bank of the estuary leading to the Atlantic from the navy base at Brest. It proceeded slowly to make no wake. The ship had no identifying markings and had no running lights to announce its presence. It was common for French warships to come and go in this fashion.

Charles was standing alone at the railing outside the bridge in the brisk morning breeze. The shore birds were beginning to squawk as the horizon behind them to the east was just starting to show the first signs of approaching daylight. He had not been to sea in several years and had forgotten how much he had missed it. He was filled by a mixture of excitement and melancholy. It was the first time he had made this passage since his fateful "day cruise" to Île d'Ouessant. His life had become complex after that with demands from his family and business. He hadn't been sailing since. Jacques Rousseau joined him at the railing to tell him that breakfast was being served in the officer's mess.

"It's hard to fathom experiencing this kind of tranquility aboard the most lethal warship ever to sail," Charles mused. "I was just imagining myself on the bridge of one of the countless sailing ships of the line that have sailed past this very point, each with more guns than their predecessor—bigger and bigger warships with more and more firepower. I suspect we are about to experience the end of an era." Both men looked forward to the calm seas and featureless horizon.

Charles finally broke the reverie, "Did you know that France deployed the first steam-powered warship in the world in 1850? The Napoléon. At 5,000 tons and 90 cannons spread over two gundecks, it had twice the displacement of the frigate we are on. It must have been an impressive sight. Perhaps it sailed past this very point."

"Have you considered purchasing another sailing yacht?" asked Jacques.

"Gabrielle gets seasick in any kind of boat," replied Charles, "but my son, Vincent, has expressed an interest in sailing and I have been thinking of taking it up again. Since the closure of NaPiles, we have been looking into some property in Saint-Jean-Cap-Ferrat. I imagine if we move there, I will have no choice but to purchase a sailboat."

Charles and Jacques went back inside and down a flight of stairs to the officer's mess. Charles slipped into the head to wash up. When he joined the others, they were standing around sipping coffee and chatting.

"Oh, Charles," Jacques said waving to Charles as he entered. "You already know the Commander and XO. I would like to introduce you to the chief engineer, Mr. Etienne Guillard. He is part of my group in Toulon and has been responsible for transferring microfusion technology from the General Research Laboratory in Grenoble to the navy base here in Brest."

"It is a great honor for me to meet the inventor of microfusion," Mr. Guillard said, stepping forward to shake hands.

"The pleasure is mine," said Charles. "You have managed a remarkable feat turning the reactors into something that can be deployed in a ship in such a short time. I would not have thought that possible."

The commander signaled for everyone to be seated and for the galley staff to begin serving breakfast. Charles said, "I'm sorry to disappoint you, Mr. Guillard, but microfusion was Cédric Rothschild's discovery. I was just a bystander."

"But you carried out the first microfusion reaction in your laboratory in Saint-Michel-de-Murienne," replied Etienne.

"Well, not exactly that either," said Charles. "I was away at my ski chalet preparing a patent disclosure. Cédric was alone in the lab at the time. He had made a slight miscalculation of the amount of deuterium to introduce, and he blew up our first reactor. It's a miracle he wasn't killed. Just ask him. He will tell you the whole story."

Etienne took a sip of coffee. "Mr. Gilbert, Sir, no one at the GRL is permitted to have direct access to Cédric Rothschild. He is completely isolated and secluded in another division."

Charles glanced over to Jacques. "Is this true?"

Jacques nodded confirmation.

"That's outrageous," exclaimed Charles. "You are keeping the greatest scientific mind of our time under wraps?"

Jacques responded, “Early on, Cédric was simply too disruptive. He kept getting into fierce debates with the scientists at the lab over his variable light-speed theories.”

“How in the world does France think it can deploy microfusion while subverting the very scientist that explains how it works?” shot back Charles.

“It’s still controversial,” answered Jacques. “The scientists in Grenoble are working out the details.”

An awkward silence at the breakfast table ensued, broken by Etienne saying, “I’m not a scientist, Mr. Gilbert. I’m just a naval systems engineer. I don’t know how microfusion works. I just know that it does. There are one hundred megawatts of propulsion power below us. In a short while, when I hit the throttle, there will be little doubt in anyone’s mind about the feasibility of microfusion turbine propulsion on ships. I was hoping to give you a tour of the reactors as soon as we finish breakfast. Once we begin the sea trial, we won’t be able to go into the engine spaces.”

“There is still plenty of time,” said the captain. “We won’t be on station for a couple more hours.”

Attempting to lighten the conversation, Jacques said, “Charles was telling me earlier about the French frigate, Napoleón, that was the first steam powered sailing ship ever built.”

After breakfast, Charles accompanied the chief engineer to the forward space in the bow two decks below. It was cramped and hot with barely enough room to squeeze between large tubes on either side of the passageway. The sound of flowing water could be heard superimposed on the sounds of machines typical of the engine spaces in a ship. "The principle of water jet propulsion is actually rather straightforward," said Etienne striking one of the tubes with his palm, resonating with a thud. "These are the twin water intake ducts for the ship's propulsion. At just ten knots, they are rather quiet, but at eighty knots, we would need hearing protection just to be in here."

"Judging by the diameter," observed Charles, "I can imagine a considerable flow of seawater must be taking place."

Etienne replied, "At maximum flow, about thirty cubic meters per second, to be exact. At the top speed of eighty knots, that's a speed of about forty meters per second with respect to the surrounding sea, which is about one half the length of this frigate per second. Obviously, the velocity of sea water in these ducts must exactly match the forward velocity of the ship. Each duct is about one meter in diameter, so the flow rate works out to about thirty cubic meters per second at top speed."

Etienne signaled for Charles to follow. "Here is an interesting feature," he said, pointing to a complex assortment of pipes and control valves. "The ship only requires the flow from one of these ducts at a time for propulsion. The second duct is for redundancy and fast acceleration. You can imagine what happens when the ship encounters ocean debris, which is an all-too-common occurrence. Sensors in the intake plenum automatically divert the flow to the second duct and a blast of high-pressure water is directed to the fouled intake plenum. This only takes about a second."

"What happens if both intakes get plugged at the same time?" asked Charles.

"That's a real problem," replied Etienne. "It's up to the operator of the bow sonar to keep the ship from encountering any large masses of ocean debris. Large schools of fish are actually the biggest concern. Now, follow me aft and I will show you the rest of the system, or at least a diagram of it."

"How did you manage such an extensive retrofit of this vessel in such a short time?" asked Charles as the two walked down the narrow corridor between the ducts.

"It really wasn't all that extensive," replied Etienne. "The original vessel was a prototype of a new class of fast frigates. It was already waterjet powered with diesel gas turbines. These were underpowered and consumed huge amounts of fuel, so the ship never performed as hoped. That is, until the diesel turbines were replaced with microfusion reactors." Turning toward Charles, he added with a huge smile, "That was a genuine game changer."

Approximately mid-ship the ducts disappeared into a bulkhead. Etienne pulled a placard out from behind a cabinet. "From here forward, there is nothing we can see. Everything is sealed up, so I will have to show you the engine spaces using this schematic." Pointing to the first element of the block diagram, "These are the twin microfusion reactors that were constructed at the laboratory in Grenoble. Everything else is pretty much standard stuff. The microfusion reactors produce superheated steam that drives the turbines that power the dynamos which are a conventional design except that, due to the enormous power output and space requirement, the windings are superconducting with liquid helium cooling." Then pointing to another portion of the schematic connected by wires, he continued, "As you can see, the two waterjet turbines are in-line with the port and starboard ducts. They are electrically powered with fixed stators. The turbine blades provide the thrust that propels the ship and are connected to steerable nozzles extending from the stern below the water line. Fifty megawatts provides more power than the ship requires to maintain constant speed, but the extra power is required for fast acceleration. If all works as planned, you will get to experience how nimble this ship is during the sea trial. Be sure to hang on."

Charles studied the diagram carefully, nodding his head slowly up and down in appreciation of the engineering elegance. It was all pretty much as he had anticipated, but more refined in practice than he had imagined. He finally asked, "So why does the reactor need to be contained in a sealed enclosure?"

Etienne responded, "There are two reasons—both of which I'm sure you will appreciate. The first is a matter of safety. As you know, in addition to the helium that comes from the deuterium-deuterium fusion reaction, microfusion generates traces of radioactive tritium. Vented to the outside, it poses no health risk, but the air enclosed in the engine compartment cannot be breathed and it cannot be allowed to leak out into the habitable spaces on board. The second reason is more sinister. You have firsthand knowledge of what happens when too much deuterium gas is introduced too rapidly."

"Ah, yes," said Charles. "The reactor will blow up. It's a failsafe precaution, then."

"Not exactly," replied Etienne. "The control systems on the reactor would never permit a catastrophe like this to happen. Rather, it's a sort of 'doomsday' scenario. Should the vessel ever be disabled or fall into enemy hands, the reactors would be flooded with deuterium intentionally to destroy them."

"And the ship?" Charles asked in alarm.

Etienne, shrugging his shoulders, "Under no circumstance could we ever allow this technology to fall into the wrong hands," he said.

The two men headed topside. "Tell me something," said Charles. "You say it doesn't bother you not knowing how microfusion works."

"Beyond natural curiosity, no," responded Etienne. "I don't know how a diesel turbine works either. All I need to know is how much thrust I get from an amount of injected fuel. It's the same with microfusion. All I really need to know is how much deuterium to feed in to get the amount of output power required. My foot is on the accelerator in either case."

As the frigate headed into open seas for the sea trail, rounding the southern coast of Île d'Ouessant and passing the Phare de la Jument lighthouse to starboard, two syndicate submarines pulled in behind, undetected at a depth of five hundred meters.

Chapter 3: 70 Knots

Charles was standing on the foredeck below the bridge. The weather forecast was for calm seas, and they were in an area of high barometric pressure. A few billowy cumulous clouds clung motionless on the horizon. It was hot so the breeze from the cool North Atlantic was welcome. Charles had been in these waters many times and he enjoyed the pleasant roll of the ship in the light swell coming from the south. He watched as crewmen launched an airborne drone that would keep an eye on the only other ship in the area—a fishing trawler about ten kilometers to the northwest—and to make a video recording of the exercise from a height of one thousand meters.

Jacques appeared at the railing above him looking a bit pale. "We are about to start. I suggest that you come inside now, or you will likely be drenched. The captain said he didn't want to have to come looking for you when you get washed overboard," he added with his characteristic ironic chuckle.

On the bridge everyone was wearing bright orange life jackets and looking grave as if heading into combat. Jacques handed one to Charles and directed him to a swivel chair out of the way in the back.

The captain requested the first officer to confirm that everything was ready and looked over at Etienne, who was manning the engine controls. Etienne gave him a single nod of the head. The klaxon sounded battle stations throughout the ship.

"Bring us to thirty knots, then," he said to the first officer, who relayed the directive to Etienne. There was a slight shudder as the vessel lunged forward belying the power of the new waterjet propulsion system.

"Thirty knots, sir," said the first officer when the ship reached the cruising speed after a few seconds.

"Forty-five knots!" commanded the captain.

"Yes, sir. Forty-five knots," repeated the first officer.

Again, the vessel lurched forward as if it would jump out of the water. The captain looked over at Etienne who said, "All systems are nominal, sir."

"I guess it's time to see what this ship can do. Sixty knots," the captain commanded.

Repeating the command, "Yes, sir. Sixty knots," the first officer said. Etienne advanced the throttle and once again the ship lurched forward. At this speed the splash over the bow began sending showers of spray over the ship.

"Right full rudder," barked the captain.

"Right full rudder," the first officer repeated to the helmsman.

The ship tilted thirty degrees to starboard and carved a trough in the sea that was unimaginable for any ship that size.

At the captain's command the ship made several zig-zags typical of combat maneuvers before coming to a complete stop. The captain surveyed the bridge crew. Those who had foreknowledge of what to expect displayed triumphant expressions—others, only shock.

“Very impressive,” said the captain. “Now that the issue of operational maneuverability is settled, let’s try that again at seventy knots. Hopefully, the ship won’t break apart. Hold on everyone.”

The first officer instructed Etienne to accelerate to seventy knots. At that speed the ship was nearly airborne, and every wave crest sounded like a giant sledgehammer relentlessly pounding the hull. Showers of spray obscured the view through the windscreen where the wipers were having difficulty keeping up. The thrill had turned to alarm for Charles. He reached down on either side of his swivel chair for the seat belts and attached himself snugly.

“Left full rudder,” barked the captain.

“Left full rudder,” repeated the first officer. The helmsman complied but was also showing signs of alarm. The ship was taking a horrific beating.

The captain said, “Come full circle, then to a complete stop.” The command was repeated, and almost in no time, all was silent again.

“Now, that was really fun,” shouted the captain exuberantly, slamming his hands on the console. “No one has ever done anything like that before in a 2,500 gross ton warship!” The helmsman was still ashen, and Charles was sure he had just cheated death. The captain said, “Bring us to twenty-five knots and take us home." The first officer repeated the command, and the helmsman was clearly relieved.

"It's time for lunch," he said. "Would anyone care to join me in the officer's mess? Helmsman, you have the bridge." Then turning he walked triumphantly away followed by the first officer.

"Permission to deploy the towed sonar array now," the first officer said as they were leaving the bridge.

"That would be a good idea," replied the captain. "The system is new, and this would be a good opportunity to check it out."

Everything in the galley was on the floor. The cook's white uniform was covered in coffee stains, but he said nothing as he dutifully reassembled the espresso maker. "I'm sorry Sam," the captain said to the cook. "That was a bit rougher than I expected."

"No problem, sir," he said, handing the captain a cup of coffee. "I'm sorry, though. You will need to drink it black. The cream pitcher did not survive the ordeal."

Charles joined the two officers in the mess while Etienne went below to consult with his engineers and check on the status of the microfusion reactors. The reactors had been tested in dry dock well beyond what was needed to cruise at seventy knots, but this was the first time it was done in practice at sea. He returned after a few minutes to the officer's mess.

"Apparently, we blew out a seal on the starboard jet and damaged the nozzle," Etienne reported. "It's not serious, but we will have to limp home on just the port jet. There was no other structural damage. This ship held together quite well all things considered."

Sam began setting the table for lunch.

"Whatever happened to Jacques?" asked the captain.

"I saw him leaning over the railing losing the last remnants of his breakfast," replied Charles. "He's not much of a seaman. He only came on this voyage because I needed an escort. I guess the Dramamine was ineffective."

"So, Mr. Gilbert, what do you think of our ship?" asked the captain.

"Very impressive," answered Charles, taking a sip of coffee.

"That's all?" replied the captain. "Just, very impressive? You experienced a navy frigate go twice as fast as any ship before it, and all you have to say is very impressive? Surely you are astonished by what your microfusion reactors accomplished today?"

Charles replied, "I'm just unclear how subjecting the ship and crew to such a pounding can serve a meaningful purpose."

"No one anticipates making an Atlantic crossing at seventy knots," replied the captain. "This frigate is designed for combat where the ability to move around quickly close to shore is critical. Rail guns are a line-of-sight weapon system. The ship needs to control the airspace close in." The captain paused, then asked, "Are you cleared to discuss the rail guns?"

"No. Not really," replied Charles.

"No matter," said the captain. "I will have Rousseau read you in later. The fore and aft rail guns will each have a firing rate of about thirty rounds per minute. The ship is designed to control the region between the shore and vessels further out. With such a deadly firing rate, this ship can defend against hordes of drones, UAVs, cruise missiles...you name it. Within the range of engagement, a few such frigates will provide an impermeable wall of defense."

"Besides speed and rapid acceleration, why do you need microfusion reactors," asked Charles.

"Endurance and power," replied the captain. "This ship can stay on station for months, if necessary, but really the most important reason is that the railguns require huge amounts of electric power. Microfusion reactors are the only know technology compact enough to generate the power requirement for sustaining such a high rate of fire."

Charles paused to reflect on this. Microfusion had been, at least in part, his invention, but this was a new twist he had not considered. Finally, he commented, "I always envisioned that microfusion would enable large ships to go long distances without refueling, like nuclear power, but without the danger. I just never imagined that the first application would be to turn a warship into a jet ski. The generation of power for electromagnetic rail guns never crossed my mind."

"I'm glad you got to witness your invention first-hand—at least the waterjet propulsion aspects," said the captain. "France has plans to build ten of these frigates. We will be able to project almost limitless naval power anywhere in the world, albeit defensive power. France is not planning an invasion any time soon." He signaled for Sam to begin serving lunch.

Charles leaned back in his chair and said, "I can see where you might defend against threats in the air and on the surface of the sea, but how about under the sea?"

"You mean from submarines, I presume," replied the captain. "There hasn't been a credible threat from submarines for forty years. Only a handful of nuclear subs are still deployed, and these by mostly non-adversarial countries. Diesel boats are useless against a ship like this with modern sonar. Anyway, we will be carrying a full suite of antisubmarine weapons that are effective against any submarines, manned or unmanned."

At this point, Capt. Rousseau staggered into the officer's mess. "Ah, Jacques," said the captain grinning broadly. "You are just in time for lunch."

The next morning, Captain Philippe Gautier entered the "chiropratique" office accompanied by an ensign from his ship.

"*Bonjour*, Capt. Gautier," the receptionist said. "Capt. Rousseau is waiting for you in the SCIF.

The two headed back without saying a word. On entering the SCIF, Capt. Gautier said, "Sorry we are early, but an urgent matter has come up, and I wanted a chance to brief you before the teleconference with the director. This is Ensign Caldera, the signal intelligence officer aboard the "X".

"Don't you think it's about time to give your frigate a proper name?" asked Jacques.

"We have something urgent to show you," said Capt. Gautier, taking a seat at the table. Ensign Caldera plugged a cable from her laptop into the video monitor. "Please proceed, Ensign."

The ensign brought up video footage on the screen. "Yesterday, we launched a surveillance drone for the 'X' sea trial, as you know. This is routine. The drone has a high-resolution camera that can see a floating bottle at two kilometers. It has a down-link to the computer onboard for quickly classifying any floating object in the vicinity of the vessel that might pose a threat to the jet intake plenum. When we returned to port last night, we were reviewing the footage and found nothing out of the ordinary beyond some floating debris. But the computer picked up something anomalous that we had missed, as you can see here," she said pointing to the video screen.

Captain Gautier interrupted, "I held a debriefing with the crew before they disembarked last night. The sonar operators who were testing out the new towed array had detected two objects in the water that they assumed were whales based on their complete silence as they moved and the sound of collapsing bubbles. The computer, however, identified them as submarines. Not just any submarines, Soviet era Shark Class submarines. Of course that's impossible. No one has seen one of these in forty years. Please go on, Ensign."

"Well, sir," continued Ensign Caldera, "the camera from the drone did pick up something unusual. What we at first thought was just a stick, turned out to be moving and the V-pattern was clearly visible. I think it was a periscope."

Capt. Rousseau exhaled with a whistle and Capt. Gautier said, "I know this sounds preposterous, but we spent all night confirming it. The computer positively identified the subs as Shark Class based on hull shape, but if they are Shark Class, then they are the quietest submarines anyone has ever observed."

There was a prolonged silence in the SCIF. Finally, Jacques said, "If there were submarines in the water—Shark Class or otherwise—how in the world did they anticipate the X frigate sea trial?"

Chapter 4: Interrogation

"Hello, Gabrielle." Charles spoke softly into the microphone wrapped around his ear. What do you think of the villa?"

"It's absolutely lovely," she replied. "The photos don't do it justice. The view of the Mediterranean is stunning. Did I mention that there is a lap pool? The only problem is that it is right next door to the Navy facility on Saint-Jean-Cap-Ferrat."

"You mean *Le Sémaphore*?" asked Charles.

"Yes. There's a lot of traffic coming and going at all hours and horns blasting and sirens. Apparently, this was what drove the previous owners out."

"That would probably explain why they lowered the price to something we can afford," responded Charles. "I'm just leaving the Officer's Club and heading to Paris by the TGV. Then I plan to catch the maglev back to Nice, and I will take an autopod and meet you at the house."

"Don't do that," replied Gabrielle. "I will meet you at the station."

"Okay. Let's plan to have dinner in Nice. I will let you know when I leave Paris. It will be too dark to visit the villa by then, anyway. *Bisou-bisou*." Charles removed the earpiece and descended the escalator to the Brest-Paris station.

At Gare de Lyon in Paris, Charles was standing on the platform for the TGV maglev to Nice when he was surrounded by four uniformed military personnel. A fifth officer commanded, "Mr. Gilbert, please come with us." One of them took hold of Charles' overnight bag.

Charles did a full 360 to realize that escape was not an option. "Am I under arrest?" he asked.

There was no answer. They went out into a light rain at dusk, where another person stood with an umbrella. They traversed the courtyard to an awaiting jet quadracopter. The officer motioned for Charles to enter and followed him up the ramp. The others disappeared into the growing darkness while the aircraft lifted off with practically no sound and vanished into low-hanging clouds.

"Where are we going?" asked Charles, looking out the window for familiar landmarks that might be visible through openings in the clouds. He figured that they were heading south by south-west.

The officer in charge made no response.

Panic began to settle in, and Charles exclaimed, "I need to let my wife know not to wait for me at the station in Nice!"

"That has been taken care of, sir," said the officer.

Charles realized that any attempts at conversation were futile and leaned back into his jump seat to reflect on his predicament.

After about an hour, Charles could tell that the quad was preparing to land by the change in the pitch of the jet engines that were swiveling for vertical flight. The craft settled down in a compound surrounded by a high wall with concertina wire strung along the top. Bright floodlights switched on as the quad touched down. The side door popped open and the officer in charge signaled with his hand for Charles to disembark. Other personnel were waiting outside. The hatch closed and, just like that, the jet quadracopter disappeared into the night sky. Charles found himself surrounded by more naval personnel—some in uniform and others in street clothes. The entourage entered the door to an adjoining building, past a heavily armed security guard. The whole affair bespoke the highest level of security. Charles was led into a featureless room with nothing but a square table and a few chairs, over which a single bare lightbulb hung on an electrical wire. He was seated in one of these chairs and was the only one in the room.

After a lengthy wait, the door opened and a man dressed in street clothes entered the room, followed by another, who pulled the door closed and stood guard. The first man sat down across from Charles, placing a thick dossier on the table. Charles could clearly read, 'Mr. Charles Gilbert', on the protruding tab.

"Did I do something wrong?" asked Charles. "I have a security clearance, you know. I just came back from a sea trial of a new top secret navy frigate."

The man across the table did not look up as he slowly thumbed through the pages of the dossier. "Did Cédric Rothschild give you a levitating pea?" he finally asked.

This inquiry caught Charles completely off guard. "I'm not saying another word," he said. "Where are we? Who are you? For all I know you are a Syndicate agent, and this is a Syndicate charade."

This outburst elicited a slight smile on the man's face. He turned his head to gesture to the man guarding the door. The door swung open and a man who had been waiting outside stepped in.

"Jacques?" Charles stood to greet his friend. "Where are we and what is this all about?"

Captain Jacques Rousseau seated himself next to Charles and replied, "For your safety, it is best that you do not know our location. As to the reason, let me introduce Stephan from the Intelligence Ministry. Stephan put out his hand. Charles took it reluctantly.

"Do you have a last name?" Charles asked.

"No. Just Stephan," he replied. "We have a matter of extreme sensitivity to clear up. Do you know someone by the name of Jean-Luc Gallatin?"

Charles glanced over at Capt. Rousseau for assurance that it was safe to speak. "To say I know him would be a bit of a stretch, but I have met him. He showed up at my door one day after France confiscated my company, NaPiles, and sent Cédric Rothschild off to Grenoble. He handed me a check for five million euros in exchange for signing over the patent rights for the microfusion invention. His check seemed real enough, so I thought nothing more about it."

"What do you know about him?" asked Stephan.

Charles responded, "Since he had my patent disclosure in his hands, I just assumed that he was one of your people."

"Have you ever heard of Ashleigh Industries?" asked Stephan.

"Of course," replied Charles. "Who hasn't?"

"So, you were aware that he is the head of that company?" asked Stephan rhetorically.

"Frankly, I expected to be driving a school bus by that time after the way I was treated by the French government. I found him rather charming, and the money was welcome," replied Charles.

"Did you know that he is an agent of the Syndicate?" asked Stephan.

"Look," replied Charles. "Unless I am a really poor judge of character, I find that possibility absurd."

"Okay, then." continued Stephan. "Let's discuss the levitating pea you received from Cédric Rothschild."

Charles was slow to respond. "I don't know what you are talking about." He finally said hoping the lie was not too obvious on his face.

Stephan glanced over at Jacques. The interrogation was over. He stood up and walked out of the room, followed by the guard, who pulled the door closed behind them. Charles and Jacques sat in silence staring at one another across the table.

"What in the world was that all about? And who is that Stephan character?"

Jacques sat motionless for a moment and then hopped up. "Let me drive you to your hotel in Nice and I will explain everything,"

"Where are we?" asked Charles.

"Somewhere in a remote forest north of Toulon. It doesn't exist on any map. You would never find it on your own," replied Jacques. The two walked out into the cool mountain air of southern France to Jacques' waiting car which had been brought up by one of the security guards. "Get in," said Jacques. "It should take us about an hour to reach Nice."

The narrow mountain road wound through dense pine forests for several kilometers. They rounded a bend and then the familiar lights of the cities along the Côte d'Azur came into view.

"Why all the cloak-and-dagger stuff?" asked Charles.

"Stephan needed to meet you in person to assess your character for himself. He wanted to see how you would react under pressure," said Jacques.

"Does he really think Gallatin is a Syndicate agent?" asked Charles.

Jacques chuckled. "No. He just wanted to see if you thought that was possible. It seems there is a highly placed mole somewhere in the French Navy. Yesterday, when we were conducting the sea trial with the microfusion propulsion, there were two submarines in the area that were monitoring our activities. The intelligence bureau concluded that they were Syndicate subs, and Stephan was detached to investigate. Someone inside the Navy that knew about the sea trial had to have tipped them off. It turns out that you were a suspect."

"Me? We both know that's ridiculous," said Charles.

"Of course," replied Jacques, "but Stephan had to be sure."

"So, what is all this about a levitating pea?" asked Charles.

Jacques smiled and looked over at him. "He knows you have it. He just wanted to be sure you would deny knowing about it."

Charles said, "Let me tell you about that thing. It has haunted me from the moment Cédric handed it to me the last time I saw him. You see, when the first reactor blew up, when he discovered microfusion, he let way too much deuterium gas into the chamber. He set off a thermonuclear detonation that should have killed him. It could have levelled the lab and left a sizeable crater in Saint-Michel-de-Maurienne. Fortunately, the bolts holding the rear cover of the reaction chamber failed, and the blast only took out the back wall of the lab and started a small fire. Blobs of molten aluminum went everywhere. While Cédric was cleaning up the mess, he noticed that one of the spherical blobs, about the size of a garden pea, did not behave normally. When it rolled off the dustpan it drifted slowly to the ground. As far as he could tell, none of the other blobs behaved this way. He knew this was a phenomenon completely outside anything known. He had a hunch, and he knew the 'pea' would not be safe in his possession."

After a while they pulled onto a thoroughfare that Charles recognized. "Do you know where we are going?" he asked.

"The *Majestique*," replied Jacques. "One of our people met Gabrielle at the train station and took her there. One of my favorite restaurants in all of Nice is in the mezzanine on the first floor."

Charles continued the story. "The nature of the levitating spherical blob of aluminum was a mystery. I suspect that Cédric figured it out, but we have not communicated since that day. At the time, our objective was to fabricate larger and larger clusters of neutrons. All we were getting were a few small clusters. One evening, I was watching my son play with a bunch of magnetic balls. He could pull a single strand out of a random cluster and then coil it into a helical tube. I mentioned this to Cédric at work the following morning, and he immediately realized that this was the solution to making more stable neutron structures. The individual strands of single neutrons were just too fragile, and once they reached a certain length, they broke apart and collapsed into a random mass, dropping down into a collection pan. Cédric began modifying the reaction chamber with a rotating magnetic field that forced the neutron strand to assemble into a tube. There was apparently no limit to how many neutrons could be assembled into these robust structures, and before long, we could actually see them with a microscope. Of course, nuclear fusion was not on our minds—at least not on my mind. We only wanted to mimic the nature of neutron stars. I called it, "a neutron star in a bottle". We really had no idea what we were doing, except, in hindsight, I suspect that Cédric was already hatching a plan to introduce deuterium into the reaction chamber. I think that's why he sent me off to my ski chalet for the weekend. He must have suspected that there was an element of risk with the experiment and wanted me out of his hair and out of danger.

In any event, his first demonstration of microfusion was compelling, and the levitating aluminum globule was just an unexpected outcome. We continued fabricating longer and longer helical structures, assuming that it was essential for the fusion effect. But it became apparent that unstructured neutron clusters worked just as well for promoting microfusion and were far easier to fabricate than our structured ones. When the French government took over the NaPiles laboratory and shipped Cédric off to Grenoble, they were only interested in microfusion and showed no interest in our ability to wind neutrons into stable three-dimensional structures. The neutron winding reactor was sent to the laboratory in Grenoble but was apparently never activated. Here's the amazing thing about Cédric's levitating 'pea'; as far as I know, it is the only specimen in existence of structured neutrons. As you know, I set up a small research laboratory in Aix-en-Provence. I recently talked to a guy at the Physics Institute to see if he might be interested in investigating the phenomenon."

"That would be Dr. Alexy Sarkova, I presume," said Jacques.

Charles flashed him a puzzled glance. "Is there anything you don't know? Anyway," Charles continued, "He had impeccable credentials in particle physics and what seemed to be an open mind. I gave him a copy of Cédric's 'Dark Matter' manuscript—Oh, I forgot to mention this in your office the other day."

"No problem," replied Jacques. "I already knew about that copy."

Charles shook his head in wonder. "Dr. Sarkova has been developing techniques for imaging single neutrons using gamma rays. I had the thought that he might be able to analyze the 'pea' nondestructively to see if the neutrons might be structured and possibly even count them. It was a wild idea, but he did not dismiss it out of hand. He understood the concept of super-massive neutron clusters and was the one that hypothesized that the neutron clusters in microfusion reactors were unstructured. That is, they are random jumbles of neutrons like what you get with the magnetic neodymium buckyballs in my son's collection when you mash them together. In this case, the net magnetic field generated by the individual spheres would be nil. This has no known impact on microfusion, but he had already suspected—perhaps he had some discussions with Cédric at the lab—that if the neutrons could be assembled in a structured way the magnetic fields would be aligned, and the bulk properties would be altered. By complete accident, during the explosion, one of these structured strands got encapsulated into the molten aluminum globule and frozen in place. Alexy confirmed that the neutrons inside the magic levitating 'pea' definitely had structure by gamma-ray analysis. But I presume you already knew all of this."

"Actually, no," replied Jacques. "Not the part about structure."

"The challenge," continued Charles, "is how to replicate the conditions that caused the neutrons to remain structured during the explosion. We were just beginning to master this after Cédric redesigned the reactor. It seems that the people in Grenoble aren't interested in this possibility, so I have been funding this research out of pocket. My pleas for support from the CNRS have so far fallen on deaf ears. And if we purchase the villa in Cap-Ferrat, I will probably have to close the lab."

"One more thing," added Charles. "Last week Alexy made a startling discovery. From the weight of the levitating 'pea' the number of neutrons inside was estimated based on Cédric's determination of the rest mass for unstructured neutron clusters. With his new gamma-ray diffractometer, Alexy was able to measure the actual number of neutrons in the 'pea'. It turned out to be six orders of magnitude less than we had thought. That means that the neutron rest mass is much greater in structured versus unstructured neutron clusters. The implications for the speed of light due to this increased mass density are tantalizing."

"How do you intend to get around the patent infringement issues?" asked Jacques.

“The patent I sold to Ashleigh only pertains to microfusion,” Charles answered, “It is silent about how the neutron clusters are fabricated or whether they are structured or unstructured. I guess if I come up with an application for structured neutrons, Ashleigh may have something to say about it, but commercialization is a long way off in any event. Can you join Gabrielle and me for dinner?”

“I best not,’” replied Jacques. “I have an early meeting in the morning, and I won’t be back to Toulon until after midnight, as it is.”

Chapter 5: The Bastion of Orthodoxy

"Go on in. He is expecting you," said the receptionist to Dr. Alexy Sarkova upon entering the executive wing of the prestigious Val d'Isère Institute of Science and Technology.

The director's office was a monument to a long and successful scientific career. Other than a desk lamp, a shaft of winter light from the south-facing window of the ancient headquarters building provided the only illumination. One wall was covered with built-in bookcases from floor to ceiling. A random assortment of books filled the shelves with volumes from friends and colleagues, various scientific and political works—most having lost relevance years ago. Conference proceedings from the past filled shelves along with multiple copies of the many books the director, himself, had written, which he handed out to visitors needing insight into a particular topic. Hardcopy books served no real purpose in the age of electronic desktop publishing, but they gave the room a warm feeling of grandeur and importance.

One wall was decorated with framed covers of some of the most significant of the hundreds of scientific publications that the director had authored, as well as a few patents, commendations, letters and photographs from important people, and various scientific achievements. A glass case behind his desk displayed awards and medals and objects accumulated over the years that recorded his many achievement milestones.

The director stood up from his desk and motioned for Alexy to have a seat at the conference table in the center of the room that could accommodate twelve people. He displayed an ample girth characteristic of an aging male accustomed to too much rich food and too little exercise. Long strands of thinning gray hair from the sides were combed over the top of his head to conceal his baldness.

"Forgive the mess," he said, pushing aside a stack of papers and manuscripts on the table he was planning to get to one day. "Whenever I go on vacation, the work just piles up in my absence." Taking his usual seat at the head of the table, the director said, "So, Doctor Sarkova, I am eager to hear how the new gamma diffractometer is working out."

"I am pleased that you are back," replied Alexy. "Things get a bit slow around here when you are gone. Thank you for approving the requisition. I know there are plenty of other equipment purchases competing for your limited funds."

The director got up to fetch the cup of lukewarm coffee from his desk. "I am excited by the prospects of the instrument. The people developing microfusion have been pestering me to develop a way to evaluate the structure of their neutron clusters."

Alexy placed a file folder on the table. "Here is the initial report. The instrument is doing pretty much what we had hoped. We are able resolve individual neutrons, albeit with the aid of a great deal of post-processing and image enhancement." Alexy retrieved a photo from the folder showing the diffuse image of what resembled a cluster of grapes and slid it across the table to the Director. "The resolution is still a bit uncertain. The way gamma rays interact with neutrons makes them appear much larger than they really are, but it is possible to estimate the inter-particle distance, in any event."

The director pulled on his glasses that hung around his neck on a lanyard and studied the image with great care. Looking up, he said, "Congratulations. This is a remarkable achievement Dr. Sarkova!"

"This is certainly the first time anyone has ever imaged a neutron cluster," replied Alexy. "It provides incontrovertible proof that the clusters are amorphous and disordered."

"You detect no structured order at all?" asked the director.

"No, sir," said Alexy, allowing the impact of the conclusion to set in. "I know the question of structured versus unstructured neutron clusters is controversial, but I think this image settles it, at least for the microfusion clusters being fabricated in our laboratory."

The director picked up the file folder and began to stand, "I am looking forward to reading your report," he said.

Alexy remained seated. "I attended a symposium while you were gone given by Dr. Rothschild."

The director sat back down. "I told them not to let that interloper speak at the symposium. He's not a doctor. He got expelled from graduate school for falsifying lab results. He's a complete fraud."

"Nevertheless, he was saying some interesting things," Alexy said.

"Like variable light speed?" shot back the director, visibly agitated by that time. "Everyone knows the speed of light is constant."

Alexy responded defiantly, "In 1491 everyone knew the world was flat and at the center of the universe."

The director dropped his glasses and stared at Alexy for a long time. "You are aware, Dr. Sarkova, that you are on the precipice of professional suicide." The words were deliberate, and his demeanor was condescending.

Alexy continued undaunted, "Dr. Rothschild, Cédric, that is, described a machine he had constructed that winds neutron strands into structured helical tubes at a company called NaPile. He mentioned a person by the name of Charles Gilbert that owned the company."

There was a long pause in the conversation, while the director sat silently fuming.

"I tracked this guy down," continued Alexy. "He corroborated what Cédric had said and gave me a copy of an unpublished manuscript called, *Dark Matter and Time-Dependent Speed of Light*."

"There is a good reason why that manuscript is unpublished," snarled the director angrily. "This Rothschild character could never get it past peer review. The paper is rubbish!"

Alexy continued, "I met with Mr. Gilbert recently to discuss the claim that Cédric had succeeded in making structured neutrons. He took a vial out of his pocket and poured out a spherical object that he called 'Cédric's levitating pea'. It drifted slowly down where he caught it in the palm of his other hand and placed it back in the vial. I was shocked and bewildered. He told me that as far as he knew, the 'pea' was the only known sample of structured neutrons in existence. He was interested in knowing if I might be able to confirm in our laboratory that the neutron cluster inside the 'pea' had structure."

"Absolutely not!" exclaimed the director. "Our laboratories are only for serious scientific investigations and not for chasing fairy tales about magic 'peas'."

Alexy had failed to tell the director that he had already performed initial investigations on the 'pea' and had a reasonable indication that the neutron cluster was, indeed, structured. He stared down at the table to avoid looking into the director's now angry eyes. "I suspected that that would be your response." Looking up, he said, "Mr. Gilbert offered me a position in his company in Aix-en-Provence, and I have decided to accept it. As of today, I am tendering my resignation from the Institute."

"What!" exclaimed the director. "Have you lost your mind? You are one of the most talented neutron scientists in the world. You wrote the definitive textbook on characterizing neutron rest mass. You have dozens of published papers, and you have been receiving invitations from around the world to give keynote addresses. You can't just throw that away."

Alexy made no rebuttal, merely shrugging his shoulders.

In a somewhat softened tone, the director said, sweeping the room with his outstretched hand. "Think what you are doing, Alexy? I had thought that you would replace me as director one day,"

"Don't you think I have been weighing the consequences of my decision?" replied Alexy. "I am forty-five years old and at the peak of my career. Now I am contemplating that everything I ever published—over 200 journal articles and book chapters—may be rubbish because they depended on the assumption that the speed of light is constant."

"This is insane," said the director. "I can't let you destroy your life like this. I reject your resignation. We will work this out."

"I'm sorry, Director," replied Alexy. "I have made up my mind. My apartment in Grenoble is up for sale and I leased a place near Aix. I have a lot of things to finish up here at the Institute, but I plan to start at Mr. Gilbert's laboratory as Research Director after the first of the year."

Chapter 6: Café Quai d'Isère

Alexy sat in a corner of the Café Quai d'Isère that he knew was frequented by the man he hoped to encounter. The man arrived right on schedule, being seated at his usual table. Alexy waited for a few minutes, then made his move.

"*Bonjour*, Dr. Rothschild, my name is Alexy Sarkova from the Val d'Isère Institute."

"Dr. Sarkova! What an honor," said Cédric with a welcoming smile. "Please join us." He pointed to the vacant chair at the table. "This is my colleague, Dr. Roberts."

"*Enchanté*," Alexy said, eagerly accepting the invitation to sit down.

"I have been following your work with great interest," said Cédric. "What a pleasure to finally meet you in person."

"You mean the gamma diffractometry?" asked Alexy.

"Yes, but mostly your work on determining the neutron rest mass," said Cédric.

"You know of my work?" asked Alexy.

"Dr. Sarkova," replied Cédric with a smile. "You are way too modest. You are one of the foremost experts on neutrons in the world. I have read your book and studied most of your papers. Your gamma diffraction ideas are intriguing, but have you considered using mesons instead? Gamma rays are massless, but mesons have mass and may work better for probing the structure of neutron clusters."

Alexy had not anticipated that his conversation with Cédric would take off in such a direction. "I considered mesons, and other subatomic particles, but they are way too short-lived to be practical," Alexy replied.

"Yes," said Cédric, "That's true of mesons in free space, but once a meson enters a neutron cluster, it's lifetime is extended by many orders of magnitude. This, of course, is why deuterons have the time needed to interact in a neutron cluster to fuse."

Alexy replied, "*Monsieur,...*"

"Please. No need for such formality. Just call me Cédric."

"This is actually the reason I needed to meet you. I am sorry to barge in on your lunchtime, but I could think of no other way to see you," said Alexy.

"Nonsense," replied Cédric. "We are colleagues and should be on a first name basis."

"I attended your symposium at the Institute a couple of weeks ago. You said some things about variable light speed that turned my world upside down," explained Alexy.

"You see, Magdalena," Cédric said, looking over at Dr. Roberts. "There was at least one person at my lecture that was paying attention."

Alexy continued, "You made mention in your talk of a former associate, a gentleman by the name of Charles Gilbert. I was able to track him down. I suspected that there was a lot more to your story than anyone knew. He confirmed everything you said. He demonstrated your magic levitating 'pea' to me and gave me a copy of your *Dark Matter and Variable Speed of Light* manuscript."

"You know, Alexy," said Cédric, "my theories are not really all that astounding—controversial, yes, provocative, yes—but rather a logical deduction from simply observing the heavens. A black hole is said to be an object so massive that not even light can escape. If true, then the light inside must be in a frozen state with velocity near zero. Thus, it is not logical that, as a black hole expands during galaxy formation, once the mass density becomes insufficient to contain it, the light leaking out suddenly takes on a very large and constant velocity. It just seems more reasonable that the velocity of light would increase monotonically without the need for this sudden discontinuity. The rest may be deduced from this simple hypothesis. The energy of a closed system is constant, of course, meaning that the product of mass and the speed of light squared must also be constant, but this does not preclude the possibility that the speed of light could be coupled to the mass in such a way that their product remains constant."

"You make the case compellingly in your manuscript," said Alexy.

"Think of the implications. If the speed of light is not a universal constant, then perhaps the universal gravitational constant is not actually constant either. Magdalena and I have found evidence that gravity is not always attractive."

"Cédric! You can't talk about that. It's classified," interjected Magdalena.

"The aspect of your theories," continued Alexy, "that has created my mental turmoil is that, if the speed of light is not constant, then all the beliefs I have held throughout my scientific career about the rest mass of neutrons, and maybe even the nature of neutrons themselves—my textbook, all my papers—are nonsense."

Cédric leaned back in his chair. "I wouldn't fret too much about this, Alexy. From the standpoint of measuring the rest mass of individual neutrons, the mass is always the same, so the speed of light seems to be constant. Not everything you wrote is nonsense. Now, the true rest mass is another matter, but where you will find a startling observation is when you try to measure the rest mass of neutron clusters. If the speed of light is constant, independent of mass, then the rest mass of a cluster should be the sum of the rest masses of the individual neutrons. With your new gamma diffractometer, I suspect you will be able to count the neutrons in a cluster. I think you are in for a very big surprise. There won't be nearly as many neutrons as expected based on the individual masses."

Alexy sat quietly, visibly shaken. "Oh my," he said. "I have been seeing this very effect and been assuming there was a calibration error."

"So there," said Cédric, jubilantly. "Now you have at your disposal an experimental means of demonstrating that the speed of light depends on mass. Is there anything I can do to help?"

Alexy took a deep breath and replied somberly. "I have resigned from the Institute. Mr. Gilbert has offered me a position in his company in Aix-en-Provence as Director of Research. He is interested in analyzing the structure of neutrons in the 'pea' and wants me to work on this problem."

"Ah," said Cédric with delight. "Charles gets it after all."

"Gets what?" asked Alexy.

"Charles realized that the bizarre behavior of the 'pea' is due to the structured neutron cluster frozen in the aluminum globule. It really pleases me to find out that you will be joining him. You know, you are committing professional suicide," Cédric said with a mischievous grin.

"You are not the first person to tell me this," replied Alexy.

The waiter visited their table after several attempts to take their food order. "Will you stay to have lunch with us, Alexy?" asked Cédric. "Now that I know your plans, we have much to discuss."

After they placed their orders, Cédric continued, "When the government confiscated Charles' company and I was sequestered at the General Research Laboratory here in Grenoble, my neutron coiling machine had been sitting idle for several months, and I was never allowed to work on it. Once they realized that microfusion did not require structured neutron clusters, sadly, my winder was disassembled for parts. I can't leave the GRL, but as soon as you get settled in Aix, I can tell you how to construct a winding machine for Charles."

Magdalena added, “You need to know, Alexy, that any dealings between you and Cédric after you leave the Institute must be carried out in secret or Cédric could get in some real trouble.”

“I think you are making way too big a deal of my gag order at the GRL, Magdalena.”

“You could go to prison,” she said.

“Let them come after me if they want,” said Cédric. “I am just thrilled to find out that Charles desires to carry on my work. Now, Alexy, I need to prepare you for life in the scientific gulag.”

“Tell me something, Cédric,” asked Alexy. “Did you really get expelled from graduate school for falsifying test results?”

This question caused Cédric to laugh out loud. “I would never falsify test results,” he replied, “but that's the gulag. Anyone that challenges the scientific order gets sentenced there by the gatekeepers of orthodoxy, who think it is their solemn duty to stamp out what they consider to be heresy. Of course, heresy is anything that does not line up with their established worldview. They will do whatever it takes to discredit you, including circulating any manner of lies. You will face this same fate if you pursue this path.”

“Is it really worth it, then?” asked Alexy.

“Only if you want to be able to sleep at night,” responded Cédric.

Chapter 7: Royalties

Charles slipped into the kitchen from the patio through the sliding door. He stood momentarily on a mat to catch the last of the drips from his wet body. He had a towel wrapped around his waist. “Wow, it is chilly this morning. I feel great. If I keep swimming laps like that, I will be a new man in no time. The pool is a bit cold, though, so I turned up the thermostat another degree.”

“Don’t you think you should wear a swimsuit in the pool, Charles?” Gabrielle said without looking up from the sink.

“The yard is private, and anyway it’s dark outside,” replied Charles.

“But they can see you from the observation deck of the Semaphore,” she said.

“I suppose if someone wanted to redirect the telescope, they might catch a glimpse of me naked. I doubt anyone would go to the trouble. Anyway, those navy sentries have much more important duties.” Charles said, heading down the hallway towards his bedroom. “I have a video conference with Ashleigh Marine at nine.”

“I’m sure you will wear a swimsuit when Vincent returns from college next week,” said Gabrielle. “I am expecting another candidate for an interview this morning. I never expected that hiring a housekeeper would be so taxing.”

The video monitor in Charles' home office came to life at precisely 9 AM. "*Bonjour*, Charles," said the man on the screen seated between two others that Charles did not recognize. "On my right is Marge Augustine, our chief financial officer and on my left is chief legal officer, Lief Trundle."

"*Enchanté*," said Charles.

"We are at the Ashleigh Marine Engine factory in Saint Nazaire to do an audit," said the man in the middle. "You called the meeting, Charles, so, what's up?"

"I am at home in Cap-Ferrat eagerly awaiting my first royalty check," said Charles.

The three looked at each other to decide who would answer. "Yes," replied Ms. Augustine, clearing her throat. "There has been a bit of a holdup. The microfusion technology has yet to be declassified. We are still waiting for approval and will not be cleared to start production for a while."

"For a while?" shot back Charles. "What in the world does that mean?"

"It means, production of microfusion reactors will be delayed," said the man in the middle.

"And my royalty payments?" asked Charles.

"The royalty payments will commence as soon as production begins," said the chief legal officer.

"This is unacceptable," exclaimed Charles. "This is going to create a huge cash flow problem for me!"

"I'm sorry," said the man in the middle, "But imagine what this means for Ashleigh. We just built a factory to make 100 microfusion reactors a month that is now sitting idle. Furthermore, cancellations for traditional gas turbine engines have been pouring in. Our entire marine division is in chaos."

"The French government can't possibly be this stupid," said Charles, massaging his temples that were beginning to throb. "Ok. I need time to process this. Kindly send me a hardcopy letter explaining the situation. Maybe the bank will be flexible with the terms of my loan."

Charles terminated the video conference without saying goodbye and switched off the monitor. He called out to Gabrielle, who was at the front door, "Will you please call for an autopod? I need to go to Paris."

"There's one in the driveway right now that dropped off the interviewee," she replied. "Do you want me to hold it?"

"Yes, please," said Charles "Let me gather some things and I will be out in five minutes."

Door to door, the trip to Paris by maglev took about the same length of time as flying. He walked outside the Gare de Lyon and hopped into an autopod.

"Where would you like to go?" said the androgenous voice.

"The Naval Directorate on Avenue Victor Hugo," replied Charles.

"Your code?"

"Gilbert 31446," he said.

The side door of the driverless vehicle on the autopod closed automatically and waited for Charles to buckle his seat belt before speeding away.

Charles dashed up the marble staircase where a security guard just inside the door said, "Please state your business."

"I am here to see Admiral Charboneau," Charles said, out of breath.

"Do you have an appointment?"

"No," replied Charles. "Just tell him Charles Gilbert would like to see him."

The security guard typed the request into the computer and asked him to take a seat in the foyer.

After several minutes, the security guard came over to Charles and said, "I'm very sorry. The Admiral is not in. Apparently, he stepped out a couple of hours ago. I suggest you make an appointment and come back."

"That's okay," said Charles, "I thought I would just take my chances." As he was walking out the front door trying to think who else he might try to drop in on, the admiral was coming up the steps.

"Charles, what a surprise to see you," he said.

"Hello, Adam. Truthfully, I came to see you. They said you were out."

"Well, I'm back now," said the admiral. "Come on up to my office."

Adam Charboneau was the Vice Admiral over the surface and undersea fleet. His office was plush, decorated with commendations and photos of ships he had commanded, although he had never been in combat. "Coffee?" he said, pouring himself a cup and one for Charles without waiting for a response.

Charles sat down on a sofa across the coffee table from the admiral who said, "So, why do I have the pleasure of your visit?"

"I was informed this morning that the microfusion reactor program is still classified," began Charles.

"That's correct," said the admiral, "and at my direction."

"Adam, how can that be? It was settled months ago that microfusion reactor technology would be released for commercialization."

"Something came up," said the admiral. "There is reason to believe that the release of the technology would constitute a security risk for the country."

"You mean the two Syndicate surveillance subs during the sea trial?" replied Charles.

"How in the world do you know about that?" the admiral asked, leaning forward and placing his cup on the table. "That's very sensitive information."

"I was on the X-frigate with Captain Rousseau for the sea trial. He told me the subs may have been powered by some type of primitive microfusion reactors and wanted to know if I thought that was even possible."

"Yes, that's the incident, but Charles, you have no business knowing about this. It's very sensitive."

"Adam, sensitive or not, if the Syndicate already has microfusion technology, that's all the more reason to declassify it and throw it open for commercial development. Keeping it secret will only give the Syndicate more time to catch up."

"That's an interesting theory," said the admiral. "I hardly see how making sensitive state secrets public could possibly serve France's national interest, though."

"Look, Adam. The reactor on the X-Frigate was built by hand at the GRL. At best, they might be able to make two a year. Ashleigh has orders on the books for 400. They are tooled to produce 100 a month."

"Ashleigh, is it?" rebutted Charboneau. "It sounds like you may have a financial motive."

"Yes, a financial motive, but since when does a financial motive nullify a sound business decision. France is the leading shipbuilder in the world. Microfusion is the single most important technology to come along for shipping since sail."

"We know this," said the admiral, "Why do you think we deployed it first on the X-Frigate?"

Charles replied, "The potential for the French economy is considerable, but I have known you for a long time, my friend, and I fear that I have failed to change your mind."

Admiral Charboneau stood and smiled warmly at Charles. "I will give what you say some thought," he said. "The next time you and Gabrielle are in Paris, Sonia and I would love to take you to dinner."

Charles walked dejectedly from the Naval Directorate and proceeded west on foot along the Avenue Victor Hugo. The earlier rain clouds had departed, and patches of blue sky were visible. After walking several blocks to clear his head, he came upon a modern structure with a small plaque on the gate that said, "French Intelligence Ministry". He thought that perhaps this might be the same agency that Stephan worked for. He pressed the button on a whim.

"Yes?" said a voice over the speaker.

"I am looking for Stephan," he said.

"Come in," was the reply, and the gate magically swung open.

He was met at the front door by none other than Stephan, himself. "I was expecting you," he said.

Charles looked around bewildered. "We have been watching you since you left Admiral Charboneau's office," said Stephan. "It was a curious twist of fate that you managed to walk past our headquarters. Please, come in."

Charles was speechless.

"Come with me," said Stephan. "There is someone I want you to meet." Climbing up three flights of stairs, they came to an office where the man behind the desk was none other than the man from the video conference with Jacques Rousseau. "Meet Abraham, our director."

Abraham jumped up and gave Charles a hug. “I was wondering if I would ever get chance to meet you in person,” he said joyfully. “You are taller than I expected from the surveillance videos.”

“Do any of you have last names,” Charles asked.

“Not ones that you will ever find out,” Stephan replied cryptically.

“The last time I met you, after hijacking me in Paris, you accused me of being a Syndicate operative,” said Charles, dryly.

“That was for show. I wanted to see how you would react under extreme duress. It was pretty easy to determine that you aren’t the type that could pull off a double existence,” said Stephan with a chuckle. “I just needed to see your reaction for myself.”

“Come, sit,” said Abraham. “I want to hear all about your visit with Admiral Charboneau. He installed jammers in his office, so we can’t eavesdrop anymore.”

Charles said, “This can’t possibly get any weirder.”

“Don’t worry, Charles,” said Abraham. “You’ll get used to it in due course of time.”

“Adam Charboneau and I are old friends. We roomed together at the Academy and have stayed close ever since,” explained Charles.

“So, it was merely a social visit?” asked Stephan.

“Not exactly,” replied Charles. “I found out this morning that microfusion technology had not been declassified, as promised. This is a financial disaster for me and for Ashleigh Marine."

"Because of the Syndicate subs during the X-Frigate sea trial?" asked Abraham.

"Apparently," replied Charles.

Stephan looked over at Abraham for approval to speak openly. Abraham nodded consent. "The Syndicate subs weren't the only ones monitoring the sea trial. We were out there with drones of our own."

"Did the captain of the X-Frigate know this?" asked Charles.

Stephan looked over at Abraham again for permission to speak. Abraham shook his head.

"What other interesting things do you know?" asked Charles.

"Well, we all know you swim naked," Stephan said with a sheepish grin.

Abraham broke into the levity, "Charles, you unknowingly wandered into a new world of subterfuge and counter-subterfuge. We have much to discuss, but it is getting late, and I am hungry. Join us for dinner and spend the night." Turning to Stephan, "I asked Cyril to prepare one more place setting. Cyril is a fabulous chef," he said.

"It's getting late, I really should be heading home," said Charles. "My wife is expecting me."

"Gabrielle will understand," said Abraham.

“You even know my wife’s name?” Charles exclaimed. “I didn’t bring any clothes, and I don’t have a hotel reservation.”

“Not to worry,” replied Abraham. “We have a comfortable guest suite just downstairs. By the way, when you talk to Gabrielle, kindly don’t mention where you are. Does Bordeaux wine with dinner suit you?”

Chapter 8: The Syndicate

"I gather that the abduction in Paris and grilling in Toulon was more than just a simple interrogation," Charles said, upon entering the private dining room.

"Let's just call it more like an interview," replied Stephan.

Abraham, Charles and Stephan were seated at a table, elegantly set with a white tablecloth and fine silverware, the plates of appetizer already in place. Cyril went around filling the wine glasses. Judging from the condition of the label, Charles could tell that the Bordeaux did not just come from the local *supermarché*.

Abraham picked up his fork and sliced off a small portion of the appetizer. "Cyril makes the best foie gras in all of France. See if you don't agree," he said, slipping the morsel into his mouth with delight.

"Can someone explain why you have been surveilling me?" asked Charles.

"Why? Because of your knowledge of microfusion, of course," replied Abraham, taking another slice of foie gras.

"I don't understand," said Charles.

"Microfusion signals the end of the petroleum age," said Abraham. "Surely you know this. For the past two centuries, world geopolitics has been dominated by crude oil—those who have it want to control those who don't, and those who don't have it want to conquer those who do. With a single fateful accident, you and Cédric Rothschild completely upset the world order. There are a lot of very powerful people that will do whatever it takes to keep this from happening."

"I'm afraid that you will need to explain what you mean," said Charles.

"Powerful interests would like to control this technology," said Abraham. "Not just petroleum interests, but miliary interests, that see microfusion as a force multiplier and business interests that see the opportunity for unprecedented wealth creation. It is in their best interests to keep microfusion under wraps. The problem, Charles, is that anyone smart enough to fire a few slow neutrons into a vacuum chamber with the right magnetic field can make neutron clusters and carry out microfusion practically in their garages. Ever since your company, NaPile, was confiscated and the technology classified, the French government has thought the secret was secure at the GRL in Grenoble. Nothing could be further from the truth. The GRL, and practically every other laboratory in the world that is carrying out what they consider to be top secret research, has been infiltrated for years by Syndicate operatives."

Abraham finished his foie gras and signaled for Cyril to begin serving the main course of sliced veal fillets, sauce bearnaise with diced carrots and julienne potatoes. "I see, you haven't touched your wine. You should try it," Abraham observed. "What do you know about the Syndicate, Charles?" he asked.

"Not much," Charles replied. "I know they are evil and behind various subversive activities."

"They are much more sinister than that," replied Abraham. "They seek world domination. The Syndicate is involved in empire building. In France they are driven by the desire to restore the Napoleonic Empire. Why they want to do this is a mystery to me, but their intention is to subvert France in the processes, and they seem to be having a lot of success doing it.

"A common characteristic of empire building is forced submission of the conquered. This typically takes the form of forcing hegemony on the conquered. The conquerors believe that if they can stamp out the cultural identity of the conquered, it will usher in peace and prosperity for everyone. Perhaps the best example of this in recorded history is given in the book of 1st Maccabees in the Bible. After Alexander the Great conquered the known world, he parceled out the conquered empire to his generals. One of them, by the name of Antiochus Epiphanes, wanted to force Greek culture on the Jewish inhabitants of Palestine under his control. He sent out a letter desiring that 'all should be one people and that each should give up his customs'. He employed great violence against his subjects to carry out this plan. That's forced hegemony. It has been practiced throughout the ages by political and religious zealots in the process of empire building. In the end, it costs them everything.

It begs the question, though: why did Antiochus Epiphanes want his subjects to be Greek? Isn't conquest sufficient? There is a common thread that runs through every attempt at empire building throughout the ages, and the Syndicate is no exception. Why did Rome want the world to be Roman? Why did the Ottoman Caliphate want everyone to be Moslem? Why did Hitler want everyone to be Nazi or the Soviet Union, everyone to be Communist? I could go on and on, but at the heart of empire you will find a charismatic leader that is surrounded by a group of loyal supporters prepared to do whatever it takes to promote the 'cause'. Unfortunately, it is almost impossible to separate the 'cause' from its leader. Empires rise and ultimately crumble under new leadership. Why? I wish I knew. There are a lot of theories, but I think the motivation for empire building is more complex than we realize. It is irrational to pursue empire by conquest. There is always a great deal of violence involved, and everyone loses in the end. It makes no sense. The Bible says, 'until now the kingdom of heaven has suffered violence, and the violent take it by force.' Perhaps there is a supernatural element that defies human logic. Why did Hitler invade Russia? Why did Putin destroy Russia to annex Ukraine? Why did China ruin their country to annex Taiwan based on antiquated territorial claims? Why did Iran subject itself to total annihilation just to annex Israel and the rest of the Middle East? More recently, why did the United States ruin their country by trying to annex Baja, California? They said it was done to prevent China from seizing the vast petroleum discoveries in the Gulf of California. I guess the rationale behind the 'cause' may have been reasonable in the beginning, but it seems that once the 'cause' fails to have clear meaning, the leadership loses their way, and the empire disintegrates.

"Where then, do I fit in?" asked Charles.

Abraham took a sip of wine and replied, "Microfusion technology offers the Syndicate a means of taking control of world energy production. You are the co-inventor. They were able to sequester Cédric at the GRL, under the pretense that they needed his scientific expertise. But you, Charles, pose a different type of threat. You slip in and out of military and business circles with ease. After you sold your patent to Ashleigh, you were supposed to join a country club and waltz off the 18th green into the sunset."

"Things didn't get interesting until you opened your lab in Aix," said Stephan. "Then Alexy Sarkova contacted you. You demonstrated the 'pea' to him and gave him a copy of Cédric's manuscript. That's when all hell broke loose."

"What do you mean? Is Alexy in the Syndicate?" asked Charles.

"Dr. Sarkova is Moldavian," explained Abraham. "As far as we can tell, he has no Syndicate sympathies, but he is surrounded by people who do. Specifically, he has a cousin that runs the PBD, the People's Bank of the Danube, the largest bank in Moldavia. This is a very corrupt enterprise involved in a wide range of subversive and money laundering activities."

Charles said, "He has resigned from the Val d'Isère Institute to come work for me. If I rescind the job offer now, he will be ruined."

"We don't want you to do that," said Abraham. "He is a valuable asset, and he brings the legitimacy to your business that you will need."

"We have been trying for years to get inside the PBD to understand how they operate," said Stephan. "They have branches around the world that seem legitimate, so it is almost impossible to follow the money flow. We have a plan that we want to propose to you. We suspect that the delay of royalty payments from Ashleigh Marine has placed you in a financial bind. We would like you to consider using Dr. Sarkova to gain access to the PBD. They have been making sizeable investments in technology start-ups throughout Europe, and they wouldn't be able to turn down an opportunity to make an equity investment in your company."

"You want me to finance my company with dirty Syndicate money?" objected Charles.

"In a word, yes," replied Stephan.

"But there is more," continued Abraham. "Microfusion technology is already out of the bag. There's not much anyone can do at this point to change the development trajectory."

"It's about the 'pea', isn't it?" asked Charles.

Abraham smiled. "Precisely," he said. "There's something about the way it defies gravity that hints at much more significant applications beyond energy production. Dr. Sarkova, coupled with advice from Cédric Rothschild, make a formidable team."

"How do you even know that such interaction between those two is taking place? They meet in secret." said Charles.

Abraham replied, "Cédric has a colleague and love interest at the GRL named Magdalena Roberts. She's one of our people. I think Capt. Rousseau may have hinted at this."

"Is Capt. Rousseau one of yours?" asked Charles.

Abraham replied, dodging the question, "There is a firewall between our respective agencies, but let's just say, we communicate from time to time. There is a high-level mole in the Navy, and we are working with Jacques to flush him or her out."

"Tell me something," said Charles. "If this is the Intelligence Ministry headquarters, where are all the people?"

"There is only a handful of staff who work in this building," said Stephan. "We have many sites distributed around the world. Centralization in the intelligence business is not a good idea."

"If I were to agree to approach this Moldavian bank, how would I proceed?" asked Charles.

"You won't be doing this on your own," replied Stephan. "We will assemble a support team. They will be transparent to you, and you will never know who they are. Once the operation is in place, I will contact you."

"You told me before dinner that I don't appear to be the type that can pull off living a double existence, and now you are asking me to be a double agent?" Charles asked ironically.

"Hardly an agent," replied Abraham, "Merely a protagonist in the story. You can leave the cloak and dagger stuff to us professionals."

Chapter 9: Magnetic Moments

Charles entered the combination on the keypad of the front door of his laboratory in Aix. He waited for the beep and click of the sliding bolt, which did not come. He was surprised to find the door unlocked and the lights on. "Hello? Is anyone in here?" he called out.

"Oh, Charles. Am I ever glad to see you! I have some remarkable things to show you," replied Alexy, coming out of the laboratory into the entry way.

"It's Sunday," said Charles. "I wasn't expecting to see you until tomorrow."

"The new 3D magnetometer showed up and I couldn't wait to try it out," said Alexy. "It is supposed to be able to map the magnetic field strength in three dimensions down to femto-teslas. I took the bag of your son's neodymium iron boride spheres from your desk to experiment with. I suspect they behave a lot like neutrons, and I have gained some useful insight from working with them. Have a seat for a demonstration.

"I am going to place a single sphere on the sample stage." Alexy pushed the 'run' button, and a color representation of the magnetic field strength appeared on the video monitor. "The colors range from red to violet, with red being the strongest field. You see the curved lines of red emanating from the north pole and curving around to the south pole. I can rotate the stage to orient the specimen however I want. Very cool, don't you think?"

Charles nodded agreement.

"Now watch," said Alexy. He opened the chamber door and placed a second magnetic sphere next to the one on the stage. They snapped together with a click. As expected, the north and south poles aligned with the axis of the two spheres, but the field strength was doubled. "No surprise," he remarked. He opened the chamber and placed a third sphere on the sample stage, which joined in the middle of the other two forming a triangle, initiated the scan and stepped back, giving Charles a chance to watch the screen and process what he saw.

"The field strength is unstable and moving around!" he said looking up.

"That's right," said Alexy. "It's almost as if the three spheres are confused about the north and south poles, which move around randomly in search of the correct orientation." Alexy opened the chamber and added a fourth sphere in the plane of the other three, forming a rhombohedron. The north and south poles immediately formed along the axis perpendicular to the plane of the spheres.

"That's amazing," said Charles. "What does it mean?"

"I haven't a clue," replied Alexy. "But I have been learning a great deal about the magnetic moments of collections of these spheres. What I have learned is that the orientation of the magnetic poles of individual spheres move around based on the field of adjacent spheres. When the number of spheres is odd, the net field is unstable and moves around. When the number is even and in the same plane, the field locks into a set direction in space." He removed the four spheres and added them to a random cluster of about one hundred other neodymium iron boride spheres on the desktop and squeezed the mass into a ball. Placing the mass on the stage and energizing the magnetometer, the field lines were sporadic and in constant motion. "You see that the cluster has some net magnetization, but with no particular orientation."

"Stay seated, Charles. Are you ready for the *coup de grâce*?" Alexy said with growing excitement. He took the cluster out of the chamber and deftly pulled a single strand of spheres from the mass, carefully wrapping the leading segment into a circle of eight balls and effortlessly coiling the strand around subsequent layers into a spiral to make a perfect toroidal cylinder. He placed the cylinder on the stage and energized the magnetometer. A bright red solid beam appeared along the central axis of the cylinder and no other color was visible anywhere in the vicinity of the specimen. "This is a marvel," exclaimed Alexy. "I would not have expected this. If neutrons are anything like these magnetic spheres, then I have just demonstrated the difference between structured and unstructured clusters."

Charles sat dumbfounded as reality began to sink in.

"There is something else I wanted to show you," said Alexy. "I took Cédric's magic 'pea' from the safe. I hope you don't mind." He demonstrated the levitating effect for Charles as the 'pea' gently drifted from the vial to the palm of his hand. "You have seen this effect before. No surprise here," he said, placing the 'pea' on the stage of the magnetometer. When activated, the same strong red beam was visible passing through the 'pea'. "I think this is pretty good evidence that whatever is inside the aluminum globule has structure similar to the cylinder I formed with the magnetic buckyballs." He removed the 'pea' from the magnetometer stage and placed it on a pan balance. "What do you read the weight to be?"

Charles looked at the digital read-out. "1,486 grams," he said.

"Now watch closely. I'm pretty sure you never observed this effect before." Alexy said as he gave the 'pea' a spin between his thumb and index finger on the balance pan.

Charles' eyes nearly popped out of their sockets. "Are you kidding me?" he exclaimed, "245 grams?"

Alexy beamed. "Let me try to spin it a bit faster." He gave it another twist and this time the 'pea' actually rose up weightlessly from the balance pan."

"How in the world did you ever discover this effect?" said Charles.

"I wish I could take credit, but Cédric tipped me off. He apparently knew about this and figured you would stumble on to it in due course." Alexy grabbed the 'pea' and placed it back in the vial. "You just witnessed antigravity," he said. "Cédric believes that gravity is not always an attractive force. I think you just saw proof of this. He has been developing a theory that links the gravitational force to magnetic fields in motion. The effect requires super-massive objects with a large magnetic moment like you observed in the magnetometer."

"Structured neutron clusters, for example," suggested Charles.

"Precisely," replied Alexy. "The magnetometer will allow us to differentiate between structured and unstructured neutron clusters. The pan balance gives us the weight of the cluster. In principle, we could calculate the rest mass of neutrons if we knew how many neutrons were in the cluster. But there is a problem. As you just saw, the weight of the cluster changes when the cluster is spinning. There is no connection to the neutron rest mass. Until very recently I thought it was important to be able to count the neutrons in the cluster, so dividing the weight by the number would yield the neutron rest mass in the cluster environment. This was the rationale behind the gamma diffractometer I built at Val d'Isère Institute. The weight of an object is a measure of the gravitational force. If the gravitational force on the cluster is not constant, then the weight is meaningless. There is a white board in the breakroom," continued Alexy. "Let's make coffee and I can explain a few things I have discovered."

Alexy switched on the light and turned on the espresso machine. "This machine is a marvel, Charles. You select the desired brew, and that's it. The machine even lets you know if you forgot to place your cup on the stage. What will you have?"

"A café latté, *s'il te plait*," said Charles, taking a mug from the shelf and handing it to Alexy. Coffee in hand, Charles sat down and Alexy went to the white board.

Alexy wrote 1.675×10^{-27} kg. "This is the accepted rest mass of a neutron. Its value has been confirmed by any number of methods. I measured it myself many times and never doubted it for one minute. I am absolutely certain that if I had a pan balance that could weigh a single neutron, this is what it would weigh. So, if I added neutrons one at a time, the weight would be the rest mass times the number of neutrons. You just observed the rest mass of the 'pea' as 1,486 grams, so if I divide this weight by the neutron rest mass, I get about 10^{27} neutrons. We both know that's absurd. Cédric told me, based on the beam flux, that he can't imagine that the cluster in the 'pea' contains more than about one million neutrons. The 'pea' weighs fifteen orders of magnitude more than it should. Obviously, the rest mass of a neutron cluster is not the sum of the individual rest masses of the neutrons that constitute it. You have no idea how difficult it has been for me to wrap my head around this." Alexy slowly sipped his coffee.

"Cédric went through this math with me at NaPiles," said Charles, "But I don't think it ever really sunk in."

"How could it?" said Alexy. "Who could possibly believe that one million neutrons could weigh more than a kilogram? And who would believe that a spinning neutron cluster could be weightless? This demolishes the very underpinnings of modern physics—that the speed of light and gravity are constant."

Charles drained his mug and went back to the espresso maker for more. "Does this disprove Einstein's claim that $E=mc^2$?" he asked

"Absolutely not," replied Alexy. "Energy is the one thing that is conserved. The energy of a neutron or a cluster of them must remain constant. The problem is that by assuming that the speed of light is constant, it means that the mass—the rest mass––is also constant. I just demonstrated that this is not the case. The rest energy is constant, but the rest mass is not. The only way this can be is if the product of mass and the speed of light squared is constant. In other words, if the mass becomes greater, the speed of light must be slower. All this involves gravity and the distinction between mass and weight."

"With this, you have gone way beyond my ability to follow," said Charles. "In any event, I came bearing some rather bad news. The royalty payments from the microfusion patent will be delayed, and we won't be able to afford the gamma diffractometer you wanted to order until the matter is cleared up."

"Actually, Charles, I don't need it anymore. Our magnetometer can differentiate between structured and unstructured clusters, Cédric told me something that made a light go on in my brain. I don't need to count neutrons after all. The quantity is not relevant. It is the speed of light inside the cluster that matters. He proposed that by observing the half-life of a short-lived particle passing through the cluster, like a pi-meson, I would be able to measure the speed of light within the cluster. We already know the mass ratio of a cluster of neutrons to the rest mass of individual ones, so according to Cédric's theories, the square root of this ratio—about 10^9—is the ratio of the speed of light in free space to the speed of light inside the cluster. The half-life of a meson in free space is about a nanosecond. In a super-massive neutron cluster, the half-life should be 10^9 times longer, or one second. This I can measure with ease. With a raster beam of columnated mesons, I should be able to resolve all the fine details of the structure of a neutron cluster just based on variations in local neutron density by the meson half-life."

"Can you really do this?" asked Charles.

"I haven't a clue," replied Alexy. "No one has ever built one. We would have to start from scratch. To begin with, I would need is a strong meson source. I think I could do the rest." He began sketching the design on the white board.

"Okay," said Charles. "What do you think it would cost to build one of these instruments?"

"Only a couple million euros. I would think," replied Alexy.

Charles exclaimed, "I don't have that kind of cash just laying around. It will take some months to raise it."

Alexy sat back down. "I have a cousin that runs a bank in Sofia. He thinks I am super smart and told me if I ever come across a really good idea, he could put me in touch with some venture capitalists he knows. What do you think? Would you like me to contact him?"

Charles pondered the possibility for a moment. "I was hoping to personally finance this lab from royalty income," he said. "The prospect of bringing in outside investors scares me, I don't want to lose control."

"With the right type of investors," losing control should not be a concern," said Alexy, "unless you make promises you can't keep. Then the loss of control will be the least of your worries."

Chapter 10: Sofia

Charles stopped by his home in Saint-Michel-de-Maurienne to be sure it had survived the unusually cold winter. Snow drifts filled the back yard, but a few crocuses were popping up in the front yard through the recent snow to announce the arrival of spring in the mountain community of eastern France. The only evidence that anyone had been inside was footprints in the walkway yet to be shoveled. He unlocked the door and walked around the empty rooms of what had been his home for the past twelve years—lost in bittersweet memories that were now fading. He found everything to be in order.

He passed by his old laboratory on the way to the autoroute and observed with some pride the NaPiles sign still over the door. The parking lot had not been plowed and the "For Lease" sign out front was practically obscured by the recent spring snowfall. A rush of memories washed over him as he remembered the series of small breakthroughs that led up to the triumphant construction of the first ever liquid sodium rechargeable battery. The happy memories were quickly overcome by the recollection of sleepless nights and anguished days when he was completely out of money and could see no way to avoid bankruptcy. It didn't matter that his battery was revolutionary, he just could not find anyone willing to take the risk of deploying something new when the old lithium-ion batteries worked well enough. He shuddered as the late-day sun dropped below the crest of the towering Maritime Alps.

His appointment with the realtor a few kilometers down the road in Modane was not until three, so he pulled into the café where he had spent countless hours trying to make the numbers work. Bills had been past due, and the bank had been threatening foreclosure. The café had brought a degree of comfort. This time was different, however. The barista was cold and indifferent. The café was under new ownership, as the former proprietor had passed away during the winter. Charles ordered his usual café latté and seated himself at the corner table that had served as his office for so many years. It was at that very table that he had met Cédric Rothschild for the first time. So very much had changed in the past two years.

"A neutron star in a bottle!" Cédric had exclaimed with the childlike delight of someone who seemed to be able to see into the future. They had invented microfusion together, but that chapter of his life was over, and his new passion was antigravity. Charles was now a wealthy man, but he had embarked on a new quest that was every bit as reckless as starting NaPiles. It would likely consume his entire fortune by the time he was done. He concluded that this time he needed to do it with other people's money.

His realtor had told him he had a buyer for his home in Saint-Michel-de-Maurienne, and Charles was eager to unload the property. He paused outside the *immobilier* to study the postings of properties for sale in the area. The prices were 30% lower than the previous year due to the global recession and even still, hardly anything was selling in that picturesque mountain valley.

His realtor saw him standing at the window and came out to greet him. "I can't believe how depressed these prices are!" exclaimed Charles.

"I warned you," said the realtor. "It's a terrible time to be selling properties in this valley. I have an offer on your home, but I am afraid you are not going to like it."

Charles ended up accepting the cash offer. Then he continued east on the autoroute to Turin where he was planning to spend the night. He would catch a flight the following morning to Sofia, Moldovia.

The delegation was seated in a semi-circle around a C-shaped table with Charles at the head. The meeting room was exquisitely appointed with Byzantine art. Ten-meter-long tapestries extended from the vaulted ceiling to the floor and swords and crossed spears decorated the walls as a reminder of Moldovia's violent past. An enormous candle chandelier hung over the center of the room, the orange LED lights and dancing imitation flames were the only things that were not authentic in the otherwise ancient venue that had served for centuries as a place where important business was conducted.

A dozen delegates were present, representing clients from family offices of the most prestigious angel investment houses around the world.

"Mr. Gilbert," began the moderator. "I have called a meeting of these delegates together on the recommendation of Dr. Alexy Sarkova. As a native son, he is highly regarded by many of us in these parts. He requested that we hear what you have to say about a revolutionary new discovery. You may proceed."

"Thank you," said Charles, switching on the video monitor behind him, "and thank you delegates. Ladies and gentlemen, I think you will find what I have to say very interesting." The word "Antigravity" came on the screen in bold letters. "I believe you will see this as the most significant investment opportunity of your lifetimes."

Charles continued, "The wheel is arguably regarded as the most important invention of all time. It dramatically reduced the amount of work required to move a load from one place to another. But the wheel did nothing to reduce the amount of work required to move a load against the force of gravity. From the time that Galileo started dropping objects off the Leaning Tower of Pisa, gravity was thought to be a constant force on the surface of the earth that was always attractive. We know from common experience that if you toss a rock in the air, it always comes back down obeying the simple laws of physics that Sr Isaac Newton codified in the Eighteenth Century. Embedded in all modern physics is the notion that gravity is a mysterious attractive force between two masses separated by a distance. Sir Henry Cavendish was the first to measure this force and place the idea that gravity was constant on a firm experimental footing. Ever since, gravity has been assumed to be determined by a universal constant, called “Big G”, that controls the motions of all celestial bodies from planets in our solar system to neutron stars.

“But is this, in fact, really true? The notion that there is a universal gravitational constant is a mere postulate. There is no proof, nor is there any way to prove it. The same is true of the assumption that the speed of light is a universal constant and has been for all time. Again, this is a mere hypothesis that until recently was never challenged.”

Charles advanced his video presentation to the next slide which asked the question “Why is gravity thought to always be attractive?” Charles continued. “Everyday experience tells us that the gravitational force is attractive. But everyday experience also tells us that the world is flat. There were people in 1492 so convinced of this that they were sure Columbus had simply not sailed far enough to go off the edge. Why is it?” Charles asked, “that all other forces in nature have directionality that can be either attractive or repulsive? Like electronic charges repel while unlike charges attract each other. Magnets have north and south poles. Why is it that gravity doesn’t exhibit similar behavior? Einstein spent his final years trying—unsuccessfully—to find a unifying theory for electromagnetism and gravity. Had he been open to the idea that the speed of light is not a universal constant, I am convinced he would have succeeded.

“I am not going to discuss the speed of light except to say that variable lightspeed is fundamental to understanding mass, and more significantly, the interaction of super-massive objects with it. Cédric Rothschild wrote an unpublished manuscript on the subject. We were working together at my company in the French Alps, when microfusion was discovered. I can't talk about microfusion here because it is classified, but an accident with the reactor we were using to wind neutrons into helical strands resulted in a globule of aluminum containing what we now believe is one of these strands. We call it a "magic levitating 'pea'". The video clip I will show you now demonstrates the antigravity effect. Let me remind you that this is confidential, and you are all under a nondisclosure agreement."

Charles showed the video clip several times in a loop. "As far as I am aware, there is no other specimen in the entire world that ever manifested this effect, the details, of which are described in a patent application that I will make available if any of you who are interested.

"This discovery offers arguably the most significant advancement in travel technology since the wheel. What it means is that an object may be lifted from the surface of the earth without expending the work normally required to oppose the gravitational force."

"What you are proposing is a perpetual motion machine," interrupted one of the delegates.

"Not at all," replied Charles. "Perpetual motion is impossible. It would violate the laws of thermodynamics. The antigravity device only modifies the extent and direction of the gravitational force. It doesn't violate any laws of physics any more than the north pole of a magnet pushing up against the north pole of a second magnet does. All the laws of physics still apply. Just to be clear, it takes work to keep the neutron strands in motion, but this work is not required to oppose the attractive gravitational force. The rotating strands merely create a repulsive gravitational force."

Charles sensed that the audience was becoming restless and hurriedly forwarded through a few slides, which he deemed unnecessarily technical, to the last slide. "What I am proposing is to build a machine that can wind neutrons into helical strands that can be embedded into rings in an antigravity device. I don't need to tell you the implications. It will be the most important and most valuable innovation of all time. Imagine a craft, like a helium-filled balloon, that can rise effortlessly from the earth. A craft without the need for wings, where the only requirement for additional power is for propulsion laterally through the atmosphere." Charles concluded with an artist rendering of such a craft and sat down triumphantly. "Are there any questions?"

A buzz ensued around the table as delegates began to discuss what they had just heard.

"Let me get this straight, Mr. Gilbert," began the delegate from Rome. "You are asking for 25 million euros to construct an apparatus that joins untold numbers of neutrons into strands that get wound into a helical coil, and you want to do this based on an aluminum globule the size of a garden pea that you claim defies gravity? What you are proposing violates all known physics and the fundamental basis of gravity." The delegate paused to take a drink of water and looked around the table at the other delegates. Then looking directly at Charles, he said, "Mr. Gilbert, have you taken leave of your senses?" This initiated a general stir around the table showing general agreement among the delegates.

A delegate from Japan said, "Mr. Gilbert, we represent many of the most important angel investors in the world. These are people with a great deal of money willing to take large risks with early-stage investments that are not yet investment grade for venture capital. But what you are proposing with your magic 'pea' could not even be classified as early-stage."

A delegate from Great Britain chimed in, "If I were to propose this nonsense to my clients, I would go to prison for securities fraud."

Charles' enthusiasm for finding an investor or investors in antigravity was dashed to pieces in a matter of minutes. The delegates began filing out of the room one by one. There were no takers. Charles sat dejected in his thoughts now that the room was empty.

There was one other person that had been seated in the back in the shadows. Charles had not observed him until he stood up and quietly walked to where he was seated. He said nothing but placed a business card on the table in front of Charles—a card with no name and only a phone number.

Charles walked slowly down the main promenade of the city towards his hotel—an unexpectedly exquisite 5-star affair a few blocks up ahead. He stopped into a café along the way to order a beer and take in the last of the warm spring afternoon. Sofia was alive and vibrant. He had always imagined the city to be somewhat squalid and a backwater, but it had become a commercial banking center, having been spared the carnage that had destroyed so many Eastern European cities during the nuclear holocaust four decades earlier.

He took a table in the sun and closed his eyes catching the last rays of sun on his face. He figured the trip had been a total waste of his time and money. He had thought the delegates would be more open-minded, but the lack of enthusiasm for his ideas was unexpected.

When his beer arrived, Stephan seated himself on the other side of the table. "Stephan! What are you doing here?"

"I hear that things didn't go so well," Stephan said with his customary frankness.

"How did you know," replied Charles. Stephan just shrugged. "The delegates were, indeed, more hostile than I was expecting."

"They are lemmings," said Stephan dryly. "They will only jump on an idea once everyone else does. The Syndicate was there to ensure that this wouldn't happen. They needed you to be discredited as a potential target for investment."

“There was Syndicate at the briefing?” asked Charles with alarm.

“Most assuredly,” replied Stephan.

“Which ones,” inquired Charles.

Stephan shrugged his shoulders. “Maybe one or two. Who knows? Just enough to ensure that none of the delegates would take you seriously.”

“So, what’s next?” asked Charles. “I need to find investors.”

“Oh, you’ll get your money,” replied Stephan.

“How do you know?” asked Charles.

Stephan patted his vest pocket.

“You mean the card in my pocket with the phone number I was given? How did you know about that?” Charles asked.

Stephan leaned back in his chair. “That’s how they operate. You will get your money—not all at once, mind you. It will come in dribs and drabs just sufficient to keep you afloat. The phone number on that card is for a bank somewhere in the world that nobody knows exists. They will ask you for wiring instructions to your bank account.”

“I don’t understand,” said Charles. “With no strings attached? What kind of investment is that? How do they get a return on their investment?”

“It’s all about addiction,” replied Stephan. “They want you to become dependent on their cash while they subvert your credibility with outsiders. It’s how they will control you. You will end up with no way out.”

"Should I stay away, then?" asked Charles.

"No," said Stephan. "We need you to get involved with them. We have a pretty good idea why they want to monopolize antigravity technology, but it is unclear how they will pull that off. You may be able to provide the key to the mystery."

Chapter 11: Neutronetics

Charles passed through the kitchen on his way back from the pool. “I see you are wearing a bathing suit,” said Gabrielle playfully.

Charles grunted and proceeded back to his room to shower without saying a word. It was after midnight when he had returned home the night before and he was unaccustomed to sleeping in. He was normally up at five, but the sleeping pills he had taken to wind down from the stress of the trip had left him groggy.

When he emerged a few minutes later, Gabrielle handed him a mug of coffee. He took a chair in the breakfast nook that was bathed in morning sunlight and selected a *pain au chocolat* from the assortment of pastries that she had laid out on the table. “You must have gotten in late,” she said. “I didn’t hear you come in.”

“There was an accident in the Tende tunnel, so I had to go clear around.” said Charles.

“How did your meeting in Sofia go?” she asked.

“Badly,” replied Charles. “I think it was probably a waste of time, but at least I got to visit our old house on the way for one last time. I accepted the cash offer. The café I used to frequent in Saint-Michel is under new management.”

Gabrielle handed him a plate of fried eggs, over easy, just how he liked them and joined him at the breakfast table.

"They assembled some of the top angel investors in the world on my behalf. Angel investors! They should understand risk," exclaimed Charles. "I have a decent track record as a serial entrepreneur, but they thought I was crazy. I think I got a sense of what Columbus must have gone through trying to raise a pile of money for a project where the armada was destined to topple off the edge of the earth into the netherworld. Sailing west to India? What a preposterous idea!" Charles took a slow sip of coffee. "Risk? I was prepared to articulate the risk of investing in antigravity. But they didn't see it as risky. They saw it as utter foolishness."

"I'm sorry, Charles," said Gabrielle. "So, what will you do now?"

"Alexy located a surplus proton generator from a hospital in Marseille. It's a steal at 1.2 million euros, but where are we going to get our hands on that kind of money? Maybe we could use the proceeds from the sale of the house in Saint-Michel and borrow the rest." Charles said gloomily. "You know, Gabrielle, it would be a whole lot easier if I just retired and took up a harmless hobby like people my age normally do. Twenty years ago, I was driven to commercialize liquid sodium batteries, and I had the vigor to do it. I don't know if I have what it takes any more to start a new enterprise."

"So, are you planning to give up pursuing antigravity?" she asked.

Charles stared out the window at the Mediterranean. "I can't understand why people are so close-minded to the idea that the speed of light may not be constant. Anyway, if I hadn't seen with my own eyes Alexy demonstrate antigravity, my life would be a whole lot simpler. I think this week I will look into making an offer on that sailboat at the marina." He reached into his shirt pocket and withdrew the card with the phone number, turning it over and over wondering about the implications.

"What is that?" asked Gabrielle.

"Oh," he replied. "Someone handed it to me after the presentation. Do you recall that I told you about the mysterious guy I met in Paris named Stephan? He showed up out of the blue in Sofia and suggested that I call this number."

"A lead, perhaps?" she asked. Charles was deep in thought and made no response.

Charles sat in the swivel chair in his office for a while before switching on the desk lamp. He fondled the card. Anxiety gripped him as he wondered what kind of murky water he might be wandering into. He picked up the phone and dialed the number.

"Hello?" said the voice at the other end after a single ring. "How may I help you?"

"My name is Charles Gilbert. I am the CEO of a company called Neutronetics. I was given this number at a briefing in Sofia earlier this week. I would like to talk to someone that might be interested in making an investment in my business."

"Yes, Mr. Gilbert. I can help you. What do you need?" said the person.

Jokingly, Charles said, "I need 1.2 million euros to purchase a high flux proton generator."

"May I have your swift code and account number?" said the person.

"I beg your pardon?" replied Charles.

"In order to execute the wire transfer," said the person.

Charles was taken completely by surprise by this. "You said, wire transfer?"

"Yes, sir. 1.2 million euros."

"You want to transfer 1.2 million euros to my account? No questions asked?" said Charles in disbelief.

"Yes, sir."

"What if I said, 5 million?"

"I couldn't do that, sir," was the reply. "That is more than I am authorized to transfer."

"But you will transfer 1.2 million euros? No paperwork, nothing?" asked a bewildered Charles.

"Yes, sir. All I need is your swift code and account number. The funds should be available in your account by the end of business tomorrow."

Charles shook his head in bewilderment, wondering what kind of transaction was going on. Providing his banking information, he asked, "How do I know you are legitimate? How do I know you won't just clean out my bank account?"

"If the money doesn't show up in your account by tomorrow, just call this number again," said the person on the other end.

Charles walked back into the kitchen. "Gabrielle, you won't believe the phone conversation I just had."

When Charles arrived at the lab in Aix, Alexy was busy uncrating the proton generator. Charles had not realized how big the machine would be—nearly two meters square at the base and one and a half meters tall.

"She's a real beast," said Alexy. "I noticed some minor damage to the enclosure and convinced the broker that it would probably require major repairs. I told him 950,000 euros was the most I was willing to pay, and after a lot of handwringing, he accepted my offer," he said proudly.

"It's bigger than I imagined. Do we have room for it?" asked Charles.

Alexy gave some instructions to the movers and motioned for Charles to follow. He had installed a rack of hydrogen tanks against the far wall and pointed to an area marked off by tape where the machine was to be placed. "The power requirements are modest," said Alexy. "The beam current is only 1 ampere, but that's enough for about a mole of neutrons per day. The neutron generator will go here," he said, pointing to another spot on the shop floor. "It won't show up until next week. The neutron winder is a bigger issue, however. I have been talking to Cédric about the design. He never built anything this large. The magnets on his winder rotated mechanically, but that's not feasible for us. We agreed that the magnet needed to be supercooled and stationary. I plan to execute the field rotation electronically, but the idea is unproven at this point. For this, I will need a top-flight engineer. I have a collection of resumes of potential candidates I would like to show you."

Charles marveled at Alexy's initiative and wondered why he had chosen an academic career path in the first place.

"Come with me," said Alexy. "I want to introduce you to Emile." Charles followed him through a double swinging door into the laboratory. Several people in white lab coats were scurrying around involved in various tasks. "Emile," he said. "I want to introduce you to Charles Gilbert, the owner of the company."

"*Enchanté*," said Emile, taking Charles handshake.

"Emile is the project manager for the neutron generator. I hired him away from the Institute," said Alexy. "He is a very capable nuclear physicist. I hired him to work out the transmutation details."

"Hired him?" asked a puzzled Charles.

"His invention is quite clever," said Alexy. "You see these rolls of gold foil? They resemble an old-fashioned type-writer ribbon. The foil passes in front of the proton beam and the gold, atomic number 79, captures two protons, transmuting into Thallium 81, and kicking out two neutrons. The Thallium isotope has a short half-life and decays back to gold giving up an alpha particle, which we can detect. This tells us the flux of the resulting neutron beam." Alexy pointed to an enclosure on the other side of the gold foil. "This is simply a block of graphite that slows down the neutrons. Ultimately this whole unit will go into a high vacuum chamber surrounded by a collimating magnet to focus the neutron beam. If all works according to plan, we should get a strand of neutrons that will feed into the winder. My biggest concern at this point is that, if the neutron beam slows down too much, it will collapse into neutron clusters inside the graphite. I guess, worst case, we could sell supermassive neutron clusters to Ashleigh for microfusion reactors."

"If the technology ever gets declassified," said Charles sarcastically.

"You know, Charles. I spent twelve years at the Val d'Isère Institute measuring the rest mass of neutrons—at least what I presumed was the rest mass based on the measured relativistic mass. It never crossed my mind that this rest mass, based on the assumption of a fixed speed of light was actually nine orders of magnitude less than the true rest mass. Even with the discovery of supermassive clusters, everyone thought that the number of neutrons involved was determined by this rest mass. Nine orders of magnitude would have been hard to miss, but the human mind is easily deceived by orthodoxy. Anyway, a mole of neutrons in a cluster with a true rest mass nine orders of magnitude greater should be measurable."

Charles had visited the facility just two weeks earlier, and the progress was astounding. It was way beyond his expectation. “What is the construction out front?” he asked.

“That’s the main gate for the security fence,” replied Alexy.

“Security fence?” asked Charles.

“I thought you knew,” said Alexy. “The landlord is installing a security fence around the perimeter. The next time you visit, you will need to upload your image for facial recognition so you can open the gate.” He pointed to the corners of the room near the ceiling. “The landlord also installed security cameras throughout the facility.”

As he drove away from the laboratory, Charles had the sinking feeling that he was no longer in charge. He decided to stop into the base in Toulon to pay Jacques a visit on the way home. They had not seen each other since the sea trial. The receptionist informed him that he was in and sent Charles back to his office.

“Charles, what a pleasant surprise,” Jacques exclaimed, getting up from his desk and giving Charles an embrace and kiss on both cheeks in the honored French manner.

“I was passing through and thought I would take my chances to see if you might be in.”

“And a miracle it is,” replied Jacques. “I returned from Brest just last night and am heading to Paris this afternoon. I was just thinking of going to the base cafeteria for some lunch. Would you care to join me?" Then he said under his breath, "We think we may be closing in on the mole."

They walked along the promenade to the cafeteria where a food line was already forming. Jacques handed Charles a tray from the stack at the beginning of the buffet line. "The food isn't terrible here, but I recommend you avoid the mac and cheese. It is probably leftover from the day before yesterday," he said with a chuckle.

"Jacques," said Charles. "I need to talk to you about my business. I think I have gotten myself into something way over my head. I need your advice."

"Anything. How can I help, my friend?" replied Jacques.

"I'm the CEO and sole proprietor of the company, and yet things are progressing so rapidly, I can hardly believe the pace of what is happening. Decisions are being made on my behalf, often without my knowledge. Something doesn't seem right."

"Back up," said Jacques. "What company?"

"Neutronetics, my antigravity business," replied Charles. "The one I started to pursue the effect of Cédric's levitating 'pea'. I think I mentioned it."

"Yes," said Jacques. "But this is the first time I knew you actually went ahead with it."

"At first, I had really modest intentions," said Charles. "I leased an abandoned warehouse in Aix-en-Provence to do some simple investigations, and the next thing I knew I was running a ten-million-euro enterprise. Rather, I should say, 'It was running me'"

"That's wonderful news," replied Jacques. "You have apparently pulled together a team of motivated and capable people. You should be proud."

Charles dismissed the compliment and continued, "When the royalty payments from the microfusion invention from Ashleigh were delayed, I look a loan against my home in Cap Ferrat. Once that money is gone, I thought I would have to shut down the operation. I tried doggedly to find investors but to no avail. They all said antigravity was a foolish fantasy."

"It sounds like you have finally landed on your feet, though," said Jacques.

"No, there's more to the story than that," said Charles. "I tapped into a very unusual funding source. I call a number when I need cash, and the funds show up in my bank account the following day—no questions asked. I feel like I am calling a drug dealer intent on feeding my growing addiction—an addiction to cash."

After lunch, Charles and Jacques walked out into the courtyard. Seated at a table drinking coffee on the veranda was Stephan.

"Stephan? Where did you come from?" exclaimed Charles.

Stephan motioned for them to take a seat at the table and snapped his fingers to get the attention of the server, who understood the prearranged instruction to bring Charles a latté and Jacques an espresso.

Charles asked, “How did you know I would be here?”

Stephan flashed a faint smile. “I hear you came up with a catchy name for your antigravity company.

Chapter 12: Downhill

Charles came in from his morning swim, tightened the belt on his bathrobe and plopped down in a chair in the breakfast nook.

"Are you feeling okay?" asked Gabrielle. "You are looking a bit pale."

"I did ten laps, and then just ran out of gas," replied Charles. "It has been a stressful couple of weeks, and I think it's simple exhaustion."

"No," said Gabrielle, "I don't like the way you look. I'm going to see if the doctor can fit you in this morning."

"I don't really think that is warranted," said Charles.

Gabrielle was already on the phone. "Perfect, we will see you at 10," she said.

The clinic was close by in Beaulieu-sur-Mer. Charles didn't care much for the place because the waiting room was always filled with sick people. He was summoned by the receptionist after a short wait and ushered into one of the examination rooms. An internist did a quick check of his vital signs. Other than slightly elevated blood pressure, everything seemed to be nominal. He took off his shirt and laid down on the examination bench for a routine electrocardiogram.

After an interminable wait on the hard bench, a doctor knocked at the door and entered the room holding his ECG chart.

"The last time we saw you was more than six years ago," she said. "At your age you should be having an annual check-up."

"I am only sixty-seven and in perfect health," he objected.

She sat down in a desk chair and scrolled the computer screen to bring up Charles' medical record with a frown, then studied the ECG again. "I am not liking what I see," she said. "I want to refer you to a cardiologist in Monaco."

The last thing in the world Charles wanted to do that day was to make the 30-minute drive to the hospital in Monaco.

Gabrielle drove him and dropped him off at the front door, where he was met by an attendant with a wheelchair. "I can walk," said Charles. The attendant shook his head and pointed him to the wheelchair. They were expecting him in the emergency room, and after some paperwork, he was signed in and wheeled into one of the examination rooms. They installed an IV, hooked him up to a blood pressure cuff, and an ECG, which started beeping annoyingly. Charles was sure that all this attention was being wasted on him.

After a while a doctor entered. "Hello, Mr. Gilbert. My name is Doctor Mailot. The clinic in Beaulieu-sur-Mer referred you—just in time, I would say. I think you are having a heart attack. Are you experiencing chest pains?"

"No," said Charles. "Other than feeling a bit run down, I feel pretty good."

The doctor reviewed Charles' medical chart again. "You are a very lucky man," said the doctor. "You probably should not still be alive. We want to do an emergency angiogram to confirm the diagnosis."

Charles emerged slowly from the fog of anesthesia. His first thought was that the clock on the wall must have stopped working. Then he became aware that he was in considerable discomfort.

Gabrielle stroked his forehead. "You gave us quite a scare," she said.

"Hi, Dad," said Vincent.

"Aren't you supposed to be at school?" Charles said.

Vincent looked over at his mom. "I came the minute I heard."

"Heard what?" asked Charles

Gabrielle took his hand. "Charles, darling," she said. "You just came out of surgery."

"Surgery?" Charles said. His mind was beginning to clear, and the distant pain was no longer so distant.

"Yes," said Gabrielle. "Open heart surgery. You have been out for fourteen hours."

"This can't be happening," said Charles.

"Your heart stopped twice during the surgery," said Vincent. "We thought we were going to lose you. But the surgeon says the procedure was successful. Thank God."

"Procedure?" asked Charles.

"Yes. You have three brand new arteries in your heart," said Vincent.

"What?" exclaimed Charles.

"Yes, darling," replied Gabrielle. "Brand new synthetic ones. They say, unlike the ones they removed from your heart, these will never get clogged with plaque."

Charles closed his eyes and groaned.

"Three days and I am getting really stir-crazy," Charles said when Gabrielle entered his room for her daily visit. "I circumnavigated the recovery wing without a walker this morning," he said. "You would think that with all the breakthroughs in medical technology, someone would have come up with a hospital gown that isn't open in the back. The doc says if I get back to swimming, I shouldn't need to attend cardiac rehabilitation classes."

Gabrielle reached in her bag to fetch an envelope. "This came by courier this morning," she said, handing it to Charles. "It is from the European Patent Office. I thought you would want to open it."

Charles tossed the envelope on the bedside table. "I am not in the mood to read more lame arguments from idiot patent examiners why they keep rejecting my claims. Someone is paying them off," he said gloomily.

At that moment a man entered the room, causing Charles to brighten noticeably. "Stephan! What a pleasant surprise.

Gabrielle, this is the mysterious guy I have been telling you about."

"Very nice to finally meet you," said Stephan, giving her an embrace as if they were old friends. "It seems that you saved your husband's life. The Agency sends its deepest gratitude."

"I will let the two of you catch up," said Gabrielle, gathering her things and giving Charles a kiss. "I will return later to check up on you."

Charles said to her, "The doctor says I can go to dinner in the cafeteria, if you supervise the excursion. See you later. *Bisou-bisou.*"

Stephan sat quietly for a minute. "Aren't you going to open that," he said, pointing to the envelope on the bedside table.

"I've been through an ordeal, and I'm not in the mood for more upsetting news," said Charles.

"I think you should open it," said Stephan.

Charles reluctantly grabbed the envelope and peeled back the flap, removing the contents with a gasp. He stared at the patent in disbelief. "It was issued!" he exclaimed. "They allowed every one of my claims. How is that even possible?"

Grinning, Stephan said, "All the examiner needed was a little persuasion from the Agency."

Charles shook his head in wonder. "Is every agency in Europe corrupt?"

"It's not like we threatened to send the examiner to the gulag," Stephan replied. "Anyway, without that patent, we were concerned that your mysterious benefactor might lose interest in your endeavor."

Charles stared at the issued patent with pride. "I ended up assigning my last patent—the one for microfusion—to Ashleigh Industries. Perhaps I will be able to hold on to this one."

"If what we suspect about the source of your funding is correct, they will try to squeeze you out of this invention before too long," said Stephan darkly.

The two sat in silence for a while to let the ramifications of the remark sink in. The only sound was the incessant beeping of his monitor, the only purpose of which it seemed, was to inform the hospital staff that the monitor was still on.

"I need to go for a walk," said Charles. "Will you accompany me?" He got out of bed gingerly, and getting some stability from the pole on wheels holding his IV drip, the two walked along slowly down the hallway without speaking.

Finally, Charles said, "I'm done. The stress of running Neutronetics is just too great. My brush with death has convinced me that it is time to call it quits."

"I think Neutronetics is a fine name for your company," said Stephan with delight, paying no attention to Charles' last comment. He pulled a paper from his pocket and handed it to Charles.

"Who is Pierre Jacquemonde?" asked Charles

"Your new electromechanical engineer," replied Stephan. "He will be able to design and build your neutron winder."

Chapter 13: The Quad

Charles stared into the video screen on the desk in his office. His morning swim had consumed nearly all his strength, and the recovery from open heart surgery was more painful and taking longer than he had expected.

"Good morning, Charles," said Alexy when the video conference began. "You look like you are doing much better this morning."

"I am still not ready to come to Aix to meet face-to-face," said Charles, "but these daily video updates are working well, and you seem to be getting on just fine without me."

"There is someone here I want you to meet," said Alexy, zooming out the camera to a wider view. "This is Pierre Jacquemonde."

"*Enchanté*," said Pierre.

"He started work last week," said Alexy. "He is highly qualified, and I am delighted to have him join our team. We have been discussing the plans for the neutron winder. The neutron generator is working well enough now that we think it is time to start making coils. He has an idea to join the ends of the coils to make hoops. The idea has merit and should result in more stable structures."

"Do you have any idea when the winder will be operational?" asked Charles.

"Most of the construction has already been done," replied Pierre. "I got a chance to meet Cédric Rothschild. He imparted to me almost everything I need to know about the design. It shouldn't take more than a couple of weeks to finish the circuitry for controlling the magnetic field. Most of the hardware components are off-the-shelf, so my job will be to write the control software."

"How will you know if it works?" asked Charles.

"Obviously the filaments are too small to see with the naked eye," replied Alexy, "and evaluating straight coils would be a challenge, but Pierre's idea to make hoops is ingenious. The hoops should generate a toroidal magnetic field that we will be able to map out in our 3D magnetometer. By the time you have recovered sufficiently to visit the lab, we should have a big surprise for you. By the way, congratulation on the issuance of your patent."

When Charles arrived at the main gate for the first time since his heart surgery, he surveyed the area for the "Neutronetics" sign he had ordered, but he did not see it anywhere. "Please pull forward a bit so the camera can see my face," he requested.

"As you wish," said the androgenous voice of the driverless autopod.

Charles lowered his widow and stared into the camera. After what seemed like an excessively long time, a message appeared on the video screen, “Access denied. Face not recognized.”

“Oh, bother,” he muttered, taking out his phone to call Alexy. “I’m here. Will you kindly let me in?” he said.

Alexy greeted him outside the front door. “I’m glad to see you. It’s been a couple of months.”

“A couple of months I would like to forget,” said Charles exiting the autopod. “I don’t see the Neutronetics sign I ordered,”.

Alexy paused to choose his words carefully. “I apologize, Charles. I overruled you. I decided it was unwise to advertise our existence. Come inside. I have something very exciting to show you.”

The complete Neutronetics team was assembled in the conference room for the occasion. Alexy handed Charles a mug of freshly brewed café latté. A model quadracopter drone was positioned in the middle of the table. “Watch this!” said Alexy, nodding to Pierre with permission to commence the demonstration. The drone lifted quietly up and hovered in place about a meter above the table.

“That’s no ordinary drone,” said Alexy proudly. “That’s an antigravity drone. The first one ever built. There are no propellers. We have replaced the props and electric motors with four rotors that have hoops made with our helically wound filaments embedded in the aluminum of the outer rim. Otherwise, the flight control is just like with an ordinary drone.”

Pierre demonstrated the maneuverability, having the drone do a full 360-degree rotation in place and then sliding left and right before completing a circle around the room and landing once again in the middle of the table.

Charles was dumbfounded. “I don’t believe my eyes,” he said.

“Here’s the thing,” said Alexy. “Once the hoops have spun up to speed, the only work required to raise the drone and fly around is to overcome the minute friction from the bearings. There is only a small battery because there is no need to move air with propellers.”

“This is a triumph!” Charles exclaimed. “You realize this will usher in the ultimate sea change in transportation.” Everyone around the table was beaming, each relishing the part they had played in the remarkable achievement of the team.

“This is just a toy,” said Alexy. “It’s now time to scale up the technology to do something practical. We have a plan to start constructing a two-seater passenger version.”

“I am so excited,” said Charles. “When do we start?”

“We are ready to go, but this will take a lot more cash than we currently have in the bank,” said Alexy.

Gabrielle came out on the terrasse as Charles was just climbing out of the pool. “Three kilometers!” he said jubilantly. “I’m almost back to form.”

Gabrielle handed him his bathrobe and said, "Alexy is trying to reach you. He says it's urgent."

Charles dried off and went directly to his office. He switched on the video monitor and initialized the video conference with Alexy.

"Charles," Alexy said. "I have some really bad news. There was a break-in last night. Someone stole the demonstration drone."

"Oh, no! What do the police say?" asked Charles, trying to synthesize the news.

"They say it looks like a highly professional operation," replied Alexy. "They think there was likely help from the inside. The security cameras had been disabled."

"Okay," said Charles, still a bit stunned. "We will recover."

"There's more," said Alexy. "The burglars apparently downloaded a copy of all our design files before erasing the drives."

"Well, surely you still have a back-up of all the files?" Charles queried.

"Of course," replied Alexy. "But someone now has details of everything we have developed."

"Even with the data files, it would take a year and millions of euros to replicate your work," said Charles. "Don't worry. We will recover."

"But Charles, this is really devastating news, nonetheless," said Alexy.

Charles said, "Okay. I will ask for more money from our investor."

He ended the call and switched off the video monitor. He removed the card from the top drawer of his desk and dialed the number.

There was a beep and a message "The number you have dialed is no longer in service." He assumed that he had misdialed and tried it again with the same result.

Charles was deep in thought when Gabrielle came into his office to tell him that his autopod was in the driveway. "Are you sure you are up to this?" she asked.

"I have no way to communicate with Stephan," he said. "The only way I can inform him about the break-in is to go to Paris in person. I packed a few things in case I need to spend the night."

Gabrielle groaned with disapproval. "At least let me go with you," she said.

"Don't worry. I will be fine," said Charles.

The queue at the Nice station ticket office was short and the trip to Paris only took about an hour and a half on the TGV maglev. A ride on the metro to a station a block away from his destination, a short walk, and he found himself at the nondescript gate of the Intelligence Ministry. He was about to press the button for the intercom when the gate clicked and swung open. He walked into the courtyard where he was greeted by Stephan. "We have been expecting you," he said. He took Charles' valise and handed it to an attendant. "Please put Mr. Gilbert's things in *chambre trois, s'il vous plait.*"

"I didn't know if you would be here, but I guess I should not be surprised to see you," Charles said, following Stephan into the building. "I have some distressing news, and I didn't know how else to tell you."

"We will take the elevator, if you don't mind," said Stephan. "Abraham is on the fourth floor, and it would be inconvenient if you were to have another heart attack climbing the stairs."

Upon entering Abraham's office, Charles saw the Neutronetics quad drone sitting on the conference table. He looked at Stephan in disbelief. "It was you who staged the break-in?" he asked.

Abraham stood up from his desk to give Charles a welcoming embrace. "Surely you didn't think we were about to let this technology fall into the wrong hands, did you?"

Chapter 14: The Health Spa

Abraham took a seat at the head of the conference table and indicated for Charles to join him. Coffee and a tray of sandwiches were on the table. "This will be a working lunch, if you don't mind," Abraham said.

"Charles, there a are a few things we need to discuss," he began. "Bear with me because there will be a lot to unpack. We would like Neutronetics to file for bankruptcy," he said nonchalantly while selecting a croissant sandwich and passing the tray to Charles.

"Bankruptcy!" exclaimed Charles. "I can't do that. I will lose my home. I took a second mortgage for 800,000 euros against it."

Abraham nodded to Stephan, who placed a sheet of paper in front of Charles, who stared at it in disbelieve. "The loan has been paid off?" exclaimed Charles, scanning the document a second time to be sure he understood it.

"Now that that's settled," Abraham said, "The Intelligence Agency is about to embark on something so secret it is beyond top secret. It is completely outside of the purview of anything in all of France. It is so secret, in fact, that it doesn't even exist—like a black hole where the gravity is so strong that not even light gets out. You can be part of this if you choose, but I will not force you into it."

Charles washed down his first bite of sandwich with coffee. He stared at the ceiling for a moment to collect his thoughts and try to figure out what he was getting himself into. Once again, he felt like he was wading into water way over his head. "I'm sixty-seven years old," he said. "Too young to have a heart attack. I'm not nearly as agile as I used to be, but my health is improving and maybe I have a few good years left. I'm not ready to take up golf or begin doing jigsaw puzzles." He finished his sandwich and took a second one. "Starting up Neutronetics from scratch has been the most rewarding thing I have ever done. I thought I could handle the stress, but now I'm not so sure. Now you want me to enter the unknown, but I'm not sure I am up to it."

"You will have an opportunity to see antigravity to completion," said Abraham. "I cannot guarantee that it will be stress-free, but I can assure you that it will be exciting."

"Can I sleep on it?" asked Charles.

"No," replied Abraham.

Charles finished the second sandwich and picked up a third one. "Okay, I'm in," he said, "but you may be dealing with a corpse if what you have in mind exceeds my abilities."

"That should not be a concern," said Abraham. "The Agency has ample resources. For one thing, your days of worrying about money are over."

"What about the antigravity patent?" asked Charles. "Now that it is published, the whole world will be able to figure out how it works."

"Did you read it carefully?" asked Abraham. Stephan placed a copy on the table in front of Charles.

"I reread the claims," Charles said, "but not the main body. There was no need."

Abraham grinned and looked over at Stephan. "You will want to read the rest of the patent carefully. We changed a few things to ensure that it could never be reduced to practice."

"What?" exclaimed Charles. "You can't do that."

Abraham flashed another grin at Stephan.

"Even if you downloaded all the design files and wiped the drives at Neutronetics, everything necessary to build an antigravity device is backed up in the cloud," said Charles.

Stephan cleared his throat and said sheepishly, "Indeed. And when completed the device will look something like a World War II B-29 bomber."

"You are not serious," responded Charles.

"With that settled," said Abraham, "We need you to liquidate the equipment at your facility in Aix. Stephan has already arranged for a broker to handle the auction."

Stepan added, "Of course we will be making the winning bid on critical equipment. Some of the easy-to-replace stuff will go to other bidders to make the auction seem legitimate."

Charles sat silently shaking his head from side to side in disbelief.

"You are going to love your new facility," said Abraham. "Stephan will show it to you tomorrow if you want. From now on, you are sworn to absolute secrecy. You must tell no one what you are up to."

"We do know how to make blabbers disappear," added Stephan with a sarcastic chuckle.

Charles could not tell from his expression if he was serious or not. "I can't do anything without Alexy Sarkova and Pierre Jacquemonde," he said.

"Jacquemonde is not his real last name," said Abraham. "In reality, he is part of our Intelligence Agency. However, Dr. Sarkova turns out to be a very interesting character. How well did you get to know him?"

"Nothing beyond casual business chat," replied Charles. "He was pretty closed up about his personal life."

"Obviously, the Agency did a deep dive into the man in order to vet him," said Abraham. "His father was killed in the Moldavian civil war and he was raised by his mother. While at university, Alexy had concluded that the Syndicate was an evil entity and got into a feud with his older brother over the matter. He worked his own way through graduate school and has remained disenfranchised from his brother ever since. The only relationship he has maintained is with his mother and a younger sister. He also has a connection with a cousin named Frederick, with whom he was close growing up. This cousin now runs an investment bank in Sofia, as you know. It is unclear if this cousin has any affiliation with the Syndicate. If so, it is well hidden. Alexy became a naturalized French citizen, which was a condition of his employment with the Val d'Isère Institute. That required a detailed background check. We don't think he poses a security risk. We are prepared to read him into the program."

"What about the rest of my team in Aix?" asked Charles.

"We suspect that one of your employees was a Syndicate mole," replied Abraham. "He or she was very careful, and we were never able to figure out who it was. You will need to rebuild your team from scratch, I'm afraid. Everyone will need to be vetted by our agency, but we have a lot of resources, like Pierre, not previously available to you."

Charles stood with Stephan at the reception desk of the Beaulieu-sur-Mer Health Spa. "I was considering joining this club one day," he said.

"Well," said Stephan, "You are now a lifetime member." He turned to the receptionist and said, "Gilbert, membership number 306, *s'il vous plaît*." The receptionist consulted a clipboard and handed Charles a towel.

Charles said, "This is all very nice, Stephan, but perhaps I can come back at a more convenient time."

Stephan made no answer and proceeded into the spa, expecting Charles to follow. The two descended into the basement utility room. There was a closet on the far wall, behind one of the water heaters, marked "Janitor". Stephan stepped up to it and stared into a small protrusion on the wall next to the door. There was a click, and the two proceeded into a long corridor. "Do you know where we are?" he asked.

"I have absolutely no idea," replied Charles.

"We are heading into the Oceanographic Institute. They recently moved to a new facility in Menton, and this one became available," said Stephan, opening a door to a large, windowless room. "This room is only about 2,000 square meters. I imagine it will serve you well for your machine shop." He pressed the elevator button, and the doors opened immediately. "There are two floors above us. There is no longer any outside access, so everyone must come and go the way we just did."

The elevator opened into an expansive concourse that Charles could immediately imagine would serve his needs very well. The facility was perfect.

"The offices are all up on the *premier étage*," said Stephan, displaying uncharacteristic pride in what he had succeeded in pulling off. "We are only two kilometers from your villa," he said. "The walk will do you good. The spa has a hot tub, infinity pool, sauna, weight room... and if you want, you can even get a massage after work."

Book II

Chapter 15: Christmas Toys

"Stephan, we need to talk", said Charles as he brusquely walked past him into the foyer. "It's been more than a year, and there is still no progress on the passenger two-seater. And, rather than getting bigger, the antigravity drones keep getting smaller and smaller. When I ask for a status update, they tell me they are working on it. All the resources are being diverted to making toy drones."

Stephan pressed the elevator call button. "It's good to see you too," he said. "You are just in time for lunch."

The two walked into the dining room where four place settings had been prepared. Jacques Rousseau stood up from the table and gave Charles a hug. "We have been expecting you," he said.

Abraham entered the dining room and signaled to Cyril to begin the lunch service. He took his usual seat at the head of the table. "Cyril prepared my favorite beef tips and sauce béarnaise," he said.

"I know it is ridiculous to inquire how you knew I was coming," said Charles. "I still have no way to contact Stephan except to simply show up at the front door where he is always waiting. And what is Jacques doing here?"

"So, what is all this flap about toy drones?" inquired Abraham, dodging the last question.

"It's been a year and there is still no progress on the antigravity two-seater. When I ask why, I get told that the engineers are working on it," said Charles. "But when I go out onto the shop floor, all I see is a production line for these tiny drones. They tell me they have a pressing need to fulfill a contract with Galleries Lafayette for stocking stuffers for Christmas. Anyway, why would we be making toy drones in a highly classified facility?"

This brought a broad smile over Abraham's face. "Perhaps the time has come to let Charles in on our little secret," he said, looking over at Stephan, who was seated next to him at the table.

"Those are not toys, Charles," said Jacques. "Those are surveillance drones."

"Perhaps you and Stephan would like to take Charles downstairs after lunch," Abraham said as Cyril and an assistant from the kitchen began the lunch service. "Your recovery from open heart surgery in just a year is quite remarkable," he said to Charles. "I was out of commission for much longer after mine," he said.

"You had open heart surgery?" Charles inquired.

"Yes," replied Abraham, "But by the time I had mine, I was seventy-five and the warrantee on all my body parts had expired. I was not nearly as motivated to recover as you have been." He took a sip of wine and added with a smile, "At my age, I think I rather prefer good French wine and fine food."

Charles was taken off guard by Abraham's frankness and did not know how to respond. There was silence for a while as they continued eating. Finally, Charles resumed the conversation and asked. "How is it possible that I have been deceived about the true nature of the activity at Neutronetics?"

"I guess the subterfuge worked pretty well, then," Stephan commented.

Abraham added, "There is quite a bit that we have kept from you, Charles, because we needed to maintain the cover you provided by deceiving you about the true nature of what was going on right under your nose. The charade has been a huge success, but I suppose the time has come to reveal the truth to you. The antigravity drones you are making, that you thought were going to be sold for Christmas presents to good boys and girls…" He chuckled at the irony of this comment, "have now been deployed widely around the world to surveil suspected Syndicate operatives. The antigravity technology that you and Dr. Sarkova developed is quite remarkable for this mission. Since the drones make no noise and have no batteries to recharge, they can stay on station undetected indefinitely. We have been inserting these tiny drones into artificial birds, like pigeons. No one pays them any attention, you know."

Stephan jumped in, "We invited Jacques because there is something else you need to know. His official role in naval intelligence is just his cover. He is one of us at the Intelligence Ministry."

Charles, in shock glanced over a Jacques, "I have known you for years! Now I find out you are a double agent?"

"Hardly a double agent," replied Abraham, "He merely works for the French Navy as his legitimate job but also works undercover for us."

"The sea trials?" Charles queried.

"That was on behalf of the Navy," replied Jacques.

"But it was a set-up?" replied Charles. "You actually invited me along to assess me?"

"Charles," said Abraham. "We have been watching you for quite a while. We needed someone with the right credentials and experience as a businessman and entrepreneur to carry out the plan. You turned out to be the ideal candidate."

"Plan?" asked Charles.

Jacques jumped in at this point. "Do you recall the conversation we had regarding Cédric Rothschild's love interest at the laboratory in Grenoble? I told you she was a plant. Her cover name is Dr. Magdalena Roberts. She is a genuine first-rate scientist, but things got a little out of hand because we did not anticipate that Cédric would fall in love with her. In any event, she was working with Cédric on antigravity theory and was keeping us informed about the progress of their work."

"Once it became clear to us that antigravity was real," added Abraham, "It was imperative that the technology never fall into the wrong hands. So, we needed to have a way to develop the technology in a clandestine fashion that would not attract the attention it otherwise deserves. Antigravity is the most disruptive technology to ever come forth."

"I think you called it, 'the most disruptive invention since the wheel' in your pitch in Sofia," added Stephan. "You have no idea what we had to go through to discredit you."

Charles placed his fork on his plate of unfinished food. "This is a lot to take in," he said softly.

"It worked, though," Stephan said. "We outmaneuvered the Syndicate and managed to field the surveillance system without their knowledge."

"The mysterious phone number?" asked Charles.

"After the break-in," replied Stephan, "The people in the Syndicate supporting your work were—let's just say, a bit agitated. Suspecting that their scheme was beginning to unravel, and with a bit of assistance from us in the form of some cleverly inserted false information, they decided to cut and run."

"What! The whole thing was just a set-up?" exploded Charles.

"And a beautiful one at that," replied Abraham.

"You used me," said Charles.

"Yes," said Abraham. "We used you to develop the most important technology in human history right out in the open without anyone ever suspecting. It was a brilliant idea. I wish I could take credit for it, but it was mostly planned by Jacques."

"And what about my heart attack that was brought on by years of unrelenting stress and sleepless nights?" said Charles.

Abraham looked intently at him with an expression that can only be described as 'fatherly'. "Sometimes greatness comes with a price," he said.

The kitchen assistant cleared the plates and retuned with a tray of desserts, which Cyril served to the four, followed by coffee.

"Ah, *île flottante*. My very favorite," said Abraham. "But don't tell my cardiologist.

"Who is paying for all of this?" asked Charles.

"You mean this lovely meal?" replied Abraham. "There are perks, you know."

"No. Everything. The drone factory. All the agents…" replied Charles.

"This all comes out of Black Ops," said Stephan. "No one knows what we do, and no one would dare ask."

After lunch, Charles, Jacques and Stephan stepped into the elevator on the fourth floor. Stephan started pushing buttons at random and Charles thought he was just fooling around until he realized that he was using the floor buttons for entering some sort of code sequence. The elevator descended and the door opened into a wide concourse filled with people seated at rows of desks. A person at each workstation was operating a joystick and intently watching several video screens.

"We are surveilling more than 1000 known Syndicate operatives," said Stephan. "And the number is growing daily. They have no idea they are being watched." He looked at one of the screens to read the location from the banner at the bottom. Turning to Charles and pointing at the screen, he said, "This is from a park bench in Odessa. There is a drone pigeon beneath it monitoring the conversation between two high-level Syndicate operatives."

Jacques interjected, "We have good news for you. In about one month, you will no longer have to enter the drone factory through the health spa. We needed to construct a loading dock for shipment of ordinary toy drones to retailers. Pallets of them will be arriving any day. As a result, Neutronetics will have a front entrance and a receptionist, so the business looks legitimate."

"Will I finally get to put up my Neutronetics sign?" asked Charles.

"Probably not," replied Jacques. "We need to come up with a less descriptive name, I think."

"Pretty impressive, don't you think?" said Stephan. "I guess we are done here. I will show you out."

"Is it still raining?" asked Charles. "I need to borrow an umbrella."

"That won't be necessary," Stephan replied. "Follow me." They proceeded down a hallway where a security guard was positioned at the end next to a door. The security guard briefly looked up at the outside security camera and pressed a button to open the door. "We are in the Montparnasse metro station. Just follow this corridor for about 50 meters. Then you should be able to recognize where you are."

"I need to retrieve my valise from upstairs," Charles said.

"No need. You will be back soon," said Stephan. "We will just place it in your room."

"My room?" asked Charles.

Chapter 16: Dark Clouds

Alexy poked his head around the corner of the open door into Charles' office, catching him flying one of the toy drones—one of the ten thousand that had arrived at the loading dock the day before.

"This is really fun," Charles said. He pressed the 'home' button on the flight controls, and the drone returned to the surface of his desk and automatically shut down. "What can I do for you?" he asked.

"I need to take a few days off to visit my mother in Sofia," Alexy replied. "She thinks she is dying and insists I visit her while she is still alive."

"So, is it serious?" asked Charles.

"I don't think so," replied Alexy. "She's a bit of a hypochondriac and every time she gets a new pain somewhere, she thinks it's the end. I need to check in on her in any event. I will be back on Monday."

"It's about time you came to pay a visit to your dying mother," Elena said.

"You are not dying, Mother," said Alexy as he walked over to the side of her bed and gave her a hug and kiss on her forehead.

"My doctors say I am," his mother replied.

"Everyone is dying," said Alexy. "They just want to scare you so you will give them more money."

“Ugh,” she exclaimed with disgust. “I would gladly give them more money if they had a cure for my arthritis so I could get out of this bed.”

Alexy’s sister came out of the kitchen, removing her apron. The two embraced warmly without saying a word. Mariam was two years younger and the two had been very close. Mariam turned away to wipe tears from her eyes. Four children came running in. “Uncle Alexy is here!” they screamed excitingly.

“Matthew,” Alexy said to the oldest boy. “How did you get to be so tall?” Matthew was reserved and gave his uncle a handshake. “And Mark? I hardly recognize you.” Mark bowed politely. The two youngest boys, Luke and John, clung to their mother, suspicious of the strange man they had never met.

“They are bashful,” said Mariam, “This is Luke, three, and John, two. Zander is running late.” Zander was Alexy’s older brother by ten years. The two had never been close. Zander studied finance and never understood Alexy’s interest in science. “Dinner is hot and ready,” Mariam said. “I suggest we not wait for Zander. Alexy, will you help me get Mother into her wheelchair?”

In her usual fashion, Mariam had set the dinner table meticulously with real candles in the candelabra centerpiece. The wheelchair was positioned at the head of the table and Alexy sat next to his mother. The chair at the other end of the table was reserved for Zander. Miriam walked around the table dishing out her famed goulash as a basket of steaming honey buns was passed.

"Sorry I'm late," said Zander as he burst into the dining room. "Frederick is being a real pain, as usual. He is a bottom-feeding carnivore when it comes to mergers and acquisitions. Hi Alexy. Glad you could join us," he said as he walked around the table kissing everyone on the cheek and hugging his mom before seating himself. The dinner conversation consisted of informal chatter about the day's highlights. Matthew made his customary rant about how much he hated his science teacher. Mark and Luke were quiet, and John was already beginning to squirm and fuss in his highchair. Mariam reported that she had just had a video chat with her husband and that his missionary project in Uganda was going well.

"So, Alexy," boomed Zander over the racket, "What have you been up to lately?"

"Not much, really," Alexy replied. "I moved into a new apartment in Villefranche-sur-Mer," he said.

"Where's that?" Zander asked, distracted by reaching for the serving bowl of sweet potatoes.

"It's a lovely village near Nice," Alexy replied.

"That's nice," said their mother.

"So how is work going?" Zander asked.

"About the same," Alexy replied. "I'm still the Chief Scientist at the drone company."

"Don't you think that is a waste of your talents?" chided Zander.

"What do you mean?" replied Alexy defensively.

"You know," said Zander. "You are a renowned scientist, and now you are working at a toy factory? I never did understand why you left the Val d'Isère Institute."

Alexy brushed off the snide putdown that was customary for his older sibling and changed subjects. "What are you up to at the bank?" he asked.

"Your cousin, Frederick, keeps throwing up roadblocks trying to scuttle the merger of the bank with Black Seas Holdings. He is asking for way more money than the bank is worth."

The remaining dinner conversation was mostly small talk about nothing very important. After dessert of tapioca pudding and coffee, Zander said to Alexy, "I need to go out for a cigarette. Mother won't let me smoke in the house. Will you join me?"

"You know I don't smoke," said Alexy.

"No problem," said Zander. "It's nice out and I need you to keep me company. It will give us a chance to catch up."

The two walked across the street and sat down on a park bench. The wilting blossoms on the trees were a sign that spring was giving way to the onset of fearfully hot summer.

Zander lit a cigarette and offered one to Alexy in vain. "Have you ever heard of a fraternal order called *Les Chevaliers de l'Égalité*?" he asked. "I think they are based in Marseille."

“The Knights of Equality? That’s a Syndicate front organization,” Alexy said with alarm.

“No, that’s just a rumor,” replied Zander. “They only seek to limit the power of globalist entities by non-violent means.”

“Yes,” replied Alexy, “So they can fill the power vacuum with their own thugs.”

Zander puffed away and blew a few smoke rings. “Mother doesn’t approve, you know.”

“Of the smoking or that you are fooling around with a subversive organization?” asked Alexy.

“Both,” replied Zander as he lit a second cigarette from the glowing embers of the first.

A pigeon next to the park bench suddenly caught Alexy’s attention as the two sat in silence. He noted that it hadn’t moved at all for quite some time. Then as he was staring at it, the pigeon glided away unexpectedly without flapping its wings. Alexy became irritated at the sudden realization that the entire conversation with his brother was being recorded in Paris.

The following Monday morning, when Alexy showed up for work, Stephan was sitting in Charles’ office. “I am back,” Alexy grunted.

“Is everything okay?” asked Charles as Alexy started walking away.

He stopped momentarily before turning around and entering the office. "To be honest," he said. "I didn't much appreciate being surveilled."

Stephan laughed, "So you noticed the antigravity pigeon? We really need to figure out how to give them some more lifelike animation—flapping wings or something."

"Have a seat," Charles said to Alexy. "Stephan and I have a matter to discuss with you."

"You passed!" said Stephan.

Alexy remained deadpan.

"You passed the test with flying colors," Stephan repeated. "We had concerns about your loyalty to France, but no longer."

Alexy sat quietly, seemingly not knowing what they were talking about. Stephan said, "We have been aware of your brother's involvement with the Knights for quite some time."

"Zander is a putz, a narcissistic putz," said Alexy.

"What is more important to us is that you recognize it," said Stephan. "In your conversation with him on the park bench you revealed an astute understanding of the true intentions of the Syndicate. I think you said something like, 'they seek to fill the power vacuum with their own thugs, once they bring down the globalists that are now in control'. That is, indeed, their intention."

Alexy said, "When I was a boy growing up in Sofia, corruption was rampant. There were shadow groups that controlled everything—drugs, weapons, money laundering, you name it. They controlled the city officials and pretty much managed everything. If anyone opposed them, they would just disappear." Alexy's voice broke slightly. "I could never prove it, but my father didn't abandon us for another woman as we were told as children. I believe they murdered him. They were ordinary thugs back then, but over time, they started acting respectably. Although we didn't call it the Syndicate, I am pretty sure that's who they became. I hate them with every fiber of my being. The way they have been flattering my totally naive brother is shameful and dangerous."

Stephan said, "I would like you to come with me to Paris tomorrow. There is someone there I would like you need to meet."

Chapter 17: Paris

Alexy met Stephan the next day at the Gare de Lyon as planned. They took the new metro that connected directly to Gare Montparnasse. Alexy did not know Paris well, so he was glad to have a guide. Stephan led the way down a narrow corridor below ground at the subway level. The only marking on the corridor was a sign that read, '*Pas une sortie*'. Stephan walked to the far end and looked up at the security camera above a door, then positioned Alexy in front of the camera for a clear view. A click, and the door opened. The security guard at the entrance recognized Stephan but asked to see Alexy's credentials before letting them enter.

"This is the flight control room for all the antigravity drones you have been making," said Stephan.

Alexy took in the sight that he knew existed but had never seen.

"Come with me. There is someone I want you to meet." said Stephan, walking up to one of the pilot consoles. "This is Melissa, she operates the pigeon drone you saw in Sofia. She is one of our best drone pilots."

"*Enchanté*," said Alexy, and looking aside at Stephan asked in a low voice, "You brought me all the way to Paris to meet a drone pilot?'

Stephan replied jokingly, "I don't think Melissa is married." She flashed him a disapproving scowl. "Come with me." Stephan said, grabbing Alexy by the arm.

They crossed the concourse to the waiting elevator, and Stephan pressed the 'door close' button. Getting off on the fourth floor, Stephan led the way to Abraham's office.

"Dr. Sarkova, what an honor," said Abraham, springing up from his desk. "Come sit. Coffee?" he said pointing to a chair at the conference table. Stephan exited the room and pulled the door closed behind him. "I am Abraham, the director. May I call you Alexy?"

Alexy was unable to speak. He had heard rumors that a guy named 'Abraham' ran the Agency, but never dreamed he would meet him face to face. Abraham's long white hair reminded him of Gandolph in Lord of the Rings. "Yes," he finally said. "Please call me Alexy."

"I have read your dossier," said Abraham. "But tell me something about yourself."

"What do you want to know?" asked Alexy.

"Start at the beginning, perhaps. I will stop you if it becomes too much," replied Abraham.

"I was born in Sofia shortly after the Great War," began Alexy.

"Yes, 2033, I believe," said Abraham. "Those were such terrible times. It must have been very hard for you."

"Well, of course I don't remember much. My mother sheltered my younger sister and me from most of the harsh reality. To be honest, I had a rather normal and carefree childhood. Even now that I know what was going on at the time, I had no sense of it growing up, and by the time I went to college, everything in Sofia was tranquil as far as I knew. My older brother was some sort of freedom fighter in the Moldavian Civil War. I remember him coming home late at night, dirty and smelly, and hiding an assortment of weapons under the floorboards. But this was practically my only exposure to the dark side of the times. My father disappeared when I was six. My mother made all kinds of excuses for his absence, but by the time I was a teenager, she said he had gone off with another woman. I knew this was a lie, but we never discussed the matter further."

"What do you think happened to him?" asked Abraham.

"I am pretty sure he was murdered," replied Alexy.

"Murdered?" mused Abraham rhetorically.

"Yes, murdered," repeated Alexy. "After the Great War, bands of warring factions formed and there was a lot of violence. I am pretty sure my father was somehow caught up in that."

Abraham sipped his coffee quietly in contemplation before speaking. "Eastern Europe was decimated by the carnage of the nuclear holocaust. Russia experienced the worst of it. Miraculously, France was mostly spared, but Great Britain and America did not fare so well. So, please, go on. You finished college at the top of your class and entered graduate school in Zurich to study physics."

"Yes," replied Alexy. "I ended up focused on particle physics and developed a clever way to measure the rest mass of neutrons for my doctoral thesis. I earned some notoriety from a couple of journal articles I published. I was hired by the Val d'Isèrè Institute as a post-doc, and that turned into a career. That is, until I attended a lecture by a guy named Cédric Rothschild."

"You caught the scent of antigravity," suggested Abraham.

"Yes, sir, and it has stalked me relentlessly ever since," replied Alexy with a grin.

"Let's rewind," said Abraham. "You said your older brother was a freedom fighter?"

"Yes," replied Alexy. "At least, that's what he called it. He was caught up in some sort of cartel that was battling other cartels for control of our sector of Sofia in the power vacuum left over from the War. To be honest, my brother, Zander, is a delusional idiot. He was addicted to the adrenalin he got from the violence. I'm not sure he ever grew out of it. Now he's flirting with the fraternal organization, Knights of Equality."

"Yes, I know this organization," said Abraham. "They are a Syndicate front."

"Zander thinks it is a false rumor," replied Alexy.

"Oh, it's no false rumor," said Abraham. He drained his mug of coffee and poured himself another, offering a refill to

Alexy, who declined it. "There is something I need to tell you, Alexy. I knew you father."

"You knew my father?" exclaimed Alexy.

"Yes. We worked together in the underground. He was betrayed by a turncoat and executed, just as you suspected."

Alexy leaned forward in his chair. "Does my mother know this?"

"I don't think so," replied Abraham, "But had she known the truth, it would have endangered you and your younger sister."

"How do you know that?" asked Alexy.

Abraham got up from his chair and went to his desk, removing a letter from one of the top drawers. He placed the discolored and water-stained letter on the conference table in front of Alexy and walked out of the office.

Alexy read the letter from his father, Alexander, to his mother.

My dearest Elena,

It seems that I was betrayed by someone. I don't know who. I am now on the run, but I can see no way of escape at this point. I am deeply sorry for bringing this misery on you and the family. Please take care of Alexy and Mariam. I have lost touch with Zander, but he is old enough now to take care of himself. I have given this letter to someone I trust. I hope it finds you well.

Love,
Alexander

Alexy shot up from his chair and rushed out into the hallway. "Abraham! Where did you get this letter?" he called out.

"Abraham just left the building with Stephan," said the receptionist.

"When will they be back?" asked Alexy.

"I think they left for the day," said the receptionist.

Alexy returned to Abraham's office and sat back down trying to figure out what to do. It seemed so strange that Stephan and Abraham would simply leave him. Finally, after about thirty minutes of waiting, he carefully folded the letter along the preexisting creases and placed it in his pocket. "What is the code for the elevator to go to the basement," he asked the receptionist.

"I can't give you the code, but I will enter it for you," he said, stepping into the elevator and punching the sequence with his back to Alexy. "There," he said, stepping back out. "Have a nice day."

Alexy walked briskly to the exit at the far end of the concourse. Melissa turned and gave him a disarming smile as he walked by.

Chapter 18: Career Change

The purple line was the first new construction project for the Paris Metro in half a century. It ran from Pont de Sèvres in the southwest to Champs-sur-Marne east of Paris, with intermediate stops at Gare Montparnasse, Gare de Lyon and Chateau de Versailles. The subway employed a whole new concept, called portals, that involved cylindrical cars that looked like commercial aircraft without wings travelling in tubular tunnels that were evacuated to eliminate the drag due to air resistance.

Alexy checked the route map on the wall to be sure he was taking the east-bound line to Gare de Lyon. There was no conventional train platform and no sound of arriving trains. Rather, the entry and exit points on the platform resembled elevator doors. Arriving trains, called capsules, could be seen through windows in the sliding doors. Upon arrival of a capsule, there was the sound of air decompressing in the airlock and the doors slid open for passengers to get in and out in the customary fashion for subways. The concept had been successful, and in time, all the Paris subways would be converted to portals, but this would require boring new tunnel shafts one hundred meters deeper, so as not to interrupt service on the existing lines.

Alexy exited at Gare de Lyon and took the elevator to the street level to the platforms where the sleek TGV maglev trains stood in neat rows. Except that the trains were exceptionally fast–

–approaching 0.8 times the speed of sound—little had changed in the way trains came and went from the station. Alexy consulted his smart phone for the correct platform for his reservation on the south bound train to Nice and found his coach.

He was not early, as the train was scheduled to depart in only ten more minutes, but it seemed strange that he was the only passenger in his coach. He was becoming anxious that there was no one else in his coach, which should have been filled to capacity by that time. He stood up to check that he had gotten on the right train when it began departing from the station.

He sat back down to watch the Paris suburbs pass by faster and faster as the train accelerated to its cruising speed.

"Is this seat taken?" came a voice from behind him.

Stephan seated himself next to Alexy. "I thought this trip would give us an opportunity to chat in privacy," said Stephan.

"How is it that we are the only ones in this coach," Alexy asked.

Stephan replied, "When you know people, it is a simple matter to just have them an extra car to the train."

"A private coach?" Alexy said with intrigue.

"Indeed," said Stephan. "So, tell me what's next for you?"

"I'm exhausted and confused by everything that happened today," replied Alexy. "I am looking forward to a glass of rosé and a warm shower in my apartment in Villefranche and going to bed early. Why did you and Abraham abandon me today?"

Stephan did not respond to this question. "I mean, what's in store for you long term?" he repeated.

Alexy took a deep breath and exhaled. "To be perfectly frank, Stephan, I am completely burned out. I have done about as much as I can do at Neutronetics. Now that I have completed the antigravity micro-engine, I am ready to move on. I have been planning to tender my resignation for a few weeks."

"What were you thinking of doing after that?" asked Stephan.

"I don't know," replied Alexy. "I just think the time has come for me to do something different—maybe try to obtain a teaching position somewhere."

Stephan reflected on this, then asked "Are you ready for a new adventure?"

Alexy turned his head toward Stephan trying to decipher the intent behind the question. Stephan's cryptic expression revealed nothing.

"Okay, you have my attention," Alexy said.

Stephan stared straight ahead. There was a long moment of silence as Alexy waited eagerly for an answer. "How would you like to have a role in bringing down the Syndicate?" Stephan said finally.

"Oh, how I hate them," said Alexy. "Especially now that I have confirmation that they murdered my father. I would love to help take them down."

Stephan was silent while Alexy dealt with the whirlwind of thoughts coursing through his mind at that moment.

"What could I possibly do?" Alexy said rhetorically. "I'm just a lowly research scientist that can't even talk about his work."

"Perfect!" said Stephan "That's exactly how I was hoping you would respond. But before you will be useful to the cause, we will need to redirect your hatred for the Syndicate into a more productive channel."

Alexy sat quietly for a while as the French countryside slipped by at one thousand kilometers per hour. Summer was approaching, so the sun was still high in the sky at 5 in the afternoon. "So, what would be the implications if I were to do this?" he asked.

"You will need to leave Neutronetics," said Stephan. "But rather than resigning, it would be best if you were to be fired for some grievous infraction—embezzling has a nice ring to it. You would need to admit that your pursuit of antigravity was fraudulent from the beginning. You would need to be stripped of every bit of self-respect in the eyes of the scientific community."

"You aren't serious?" Alexy replied.

"It's the only way we would ever be able to sell your cover," replied Stephan.

"Cover for what?" asked Alexy.

"We want you to infiltrate the Knights of Equality," replied Stephan.

"You want me to become a spy? Have you lost your mind?" exclaimed Alexy.

Stephan made no reply. He merely took on his characteristic satisfied grin when he had just proposed the unthinkable.

As the train slowed and pulled into the Gare de Nice, Alexy asked, "How did Abraham come into possession of that letter from my father?"

"You will have to ask him," replied Stephan. "I will be in touch."

The two parted company in Nice. Alexy caught an autopod to go home to Villefranche and Stephan caught an autopod to take him to a hangar in the civil aviation section at the far end of the Nice airport runway, inside of which was a black craft in the form of a hemisphere, waiting for him. He slid into one of the passenger seats and the pilot switched on the flight console. After a brief ground check, the pilot initiated the process for flight. The soft sound of rotors spinning up to speed could be heard through the floorboards. The craft shimmered in the hangar lights and then became invisible. The hangar doors were opened, and the craft silently disappeared into the fading light of dusk in the cloudless Côte d'Azur sky for the five-minute trip back to Paris.

Chapter 19: The Polaris Explorer

Gabrielle handed Jacques a mug of coffee. "*Crème ou sucre*?" she asked.

"No. Just black, please," he replied.

"Have a seat in the breakfast nook," she said. "There is a tray of croissants on the table."

"No thanks," Jacques said. "I am trying to reduce my carbs."

"Charles needs to reduce his cholesterol, but I suspect his diet of butter croissants for breakfast is not helping. He should be out of the shower in a minute. He just came in from his morning swim. I don't think he was expecting you," she said.

"No. I was in the area and decided to stop by," said Jacques as he seated himself at the round table in the breakfast nook. "He said he had something important to discuss and wanted to do it face to face."

"Jacques! What a pleasant surprise," said Charles, emerging from the back room. "I was planning to come to Toulon today, but you saved me the trip." Gabrielle handed him his customary café latté, as he joined Jacques at the table.

"I needed to talk to you about Alexy," Charles said, placing a butter croissant on his plate. "His mother in Sofia took a turn for the worst and he went there in a hurry. I haven't heard from him in a week, and now I am getting concerned."

"I'm sure he will contact you when he is able," said Jacques.

"He was distraught when he left. Also, he has become increasingly distant and sullen over the past few weeks. I feared he was burning out," said Charles sipping his coffee. "I tried to get him to take some time off, but he said he had to finish a project and had nowhere to go in any event. What if he has been kidnapped?"

"I'm sure it's nothing," said Jacques, "but I will look into it." He drained his coffee and got up for a refill from Gabrielle. "I have some really good news for you, Charles." Sitting back down he said, "Microfusion is being declassified."

"It's about time," said Charles.

Jacques continued, "Apparently the technology leaked out of the GRL, and the Syndicate has had it almost from the beginning. There is no longer any need for secrecy."

"Does that mean Ashleigh can start selling microfusion engines and I will finally begin receiving royalty payments?"

"Yes," said Jacques. "In fact, Jean-Luc Gallatin has invited us to the launch of his first microfusion cruise ship at the Ashleigh Marine shipyard in Saint Nazaire next week."

Charles met Jacques in Paris the following week, where Stephan joined them. He had arranged for an Agency quadracopter to take them to the shipyard for the ceremony. They were met by Jean-Luc in a corporate van that drove them to the launch site.

“She is a real beauty,” said Jean-Luc. “The first cruise ship ever with microfusion propulsion, and at 250,000 tons, the largest cruise ship ever built. Besides adding ten knots in top speed, Ashleigh will save millions in operating costs.”

The freshly painted white ship was an impressive sight. Her name, ‘Polaris Explorer’, was neatly embossed on the bow that towered six stories above them. They proceeded up several flights of stairs to a metal platform erected for the occasion. Workmen were busy removing the last of the safety blocks and checking the rigging for lowering the behemoth into the mouth of the Loire. A band was playing, and a crowd of dignitaries was assembled. Hundreds of workers that had participated in the construction in their orange jumpsuits and hardhats stood eagerly by.

Jean-Luc gave a speech to the crowd over the PA, and when everything was ready, he broke a bottle of champagne on the bow, and the ship began inching down the incline into the water—a process that would take almost an hour.

“In about a year, the interior will be finished, and she will take on passengers for her maiden voyage to America,” said Jean-Luc proudly. The christening was followed by a gala celebration at the nearby Ashleigh Marine headquarters.

“I have still received no word from Alexy,” said Charles to Jacques as they climbed back into the quad.

"Do you mind if we take a little detour to Brest?" asked Stephan.

They flew northwest, passing over the city of Brest to a remote area inland from Atlantic coast. The pilot radioed for permission to land, without which the craft would have been shot out of the sky by a surface to air missile. He hovered over the landing pad and rotated the jet engine pods for vertical descent. Several armed soldiers were standing by as the craft settled on the pad. The door dropped down, and the three made their way to the main gate where there was a series of two turnstiles. Visitors entered one at a time through the first turnstile where a security guard sat behind bullet-proof glass. Stephan went in first, passing his security badge through an airlock to the guard for inspection. The airlock was for protection against poison gas from any would-be intruder. Stephan was cleared, and he passed a second clearance document for Charles to the guard. "This is for the guy behind me," he said. The security guard pressed a button resulting in a click unlocking the second turnstile, and Stephan exited the passageway.

Charles was next. After careful examination of facial recognition and fingerprints, the security guard passed a visitor's badge back through the airlock. Jacques was the last to go through. "I have never experienced security like that before," said Charles as two escorts met them and accompanied them to the main entrance. The compound was surrounded by a three-meter-high chain link fence, topped with concertina razor wire and security cameras spaced every few meters that gave the appearance of a maximum-security prison.

Inside the door, the three were greeted by Pierre Jacquemonde. "Pierre!" exclaimed Charles. "I have not seen you since the facility in Aix was shut down. I was wondering what happened to you."

"You are about to find out," said Pierre, turning and leading the group into a large, brightly lit, high bay factory space where several black hemispherical objects were spread out over the floor. Each dome was standing on some sort of shock-absorber struts. Charles guessed that the hemispherical domes were about four meters in diameter.

The hatch on one was open with stairs extended to the ground. "Go take a look inside," Stephan said.

Charles looked in and then ventured a few steps up the stairs to get a better view. There was what appeared to be a pilot's console, and five additional seats arranged in a circle facing outward.

"I know you were hoping for a two-seater, but we settled on six instead. It is more practical," said Stephan. "Go on in, if you want."

When Charles emerged from the capsule, Alexy was standing outside the hatch. "Alexy! Where in the world have you been? You disappeared without a trace. I feared maybe you may have been kidnapped in Sofia."

"I am so sorry, Charles," said Alexy. "*C'est compliqué.*"

"What are you doing here?" asked Charles.

"We had a glitch with the antigravity rotors, and I came here to help work help on," replied Alexy.

"We? Who is we?" asked Charles.

Alexy looked at Stephan to help him out.

"Charles," said Stephan, "every time you asked about the progress on a two-seater, you were told 'We are working on it'. Well, they were working on it, just not in your facility in Beaulieu. They were working on it at the classified facility here."

"Good grief," said Charles in exasperation. "You built another neutron winder without my knowledge?" he asked.

"Absolutely not," said Alexy. "Your winder in Beaulieu is still the only one in existence."

"You smuggled neutron filaments, then, out of my facility in Beaulieu and brought them here?" inquired Charles.

"Settle down, Charles," said Stephan. "There's not as much subterfuge as you suppose,"

Alexy said, "The rotors for the antigravity micro-drones had a single loop of neutron strands in each rotor. This worked because the lift requirement was minimal, and if a rotor did fail, the drone would simply drift to the ground, where someone could retrieve it later. With the manned six-seater, we needed a lot more lift, so we had to stack larger strand loops on top of one another. This worked great until we discovered a weight imbalance if the loops we misaligned. We have solved the problem now and the program is back on track."

“How did you solve it?” asked Charles.

Alexy replied, “Each of the rotors spins at high speed in a vacuum enclosure to reduce drag. A slight imbalance of the rotor was inducing a wobble in the bearing supporting the rotor and causing wear. Over time, air was leaking in, and the rotor would start to slow down. Under severe circumstances, the craft could lose lift and glide to the ground. This is not an option for a manned craft if the ground is behind enemy lines.”

“Enemy lines? What in the world are you guys up to?” asked Charles, looking around.

Jacques rolled his eyes. That last bit from Alexy was too much information. “Would you care to take a test flight?” he asked.

Jacques led the way to a waiting antigravity craft, where the pilot stood guard at the side of the open hatch. Charles went in first, followed by Stephan, and then by Jacques. The pilot got in last and retracted the stairs and closed the hatch. The liftoff was practically unnoticeable and without windows, it was impossible to judge the altitude.

“This flight will last only six and a half minutes,” said the pilot.

Charles was disappointed that the test flight would be so short. However, when the hatch opened after landing, he was rendered speechless as he climbed out and realized that they had landed in the driveway in front of his house in Saint-Jean-Cap-Ferrat. After exiting the craft, he noted that it was unusually dark out. He consulted his wristwatch, which said 5:29 in the afternoon. The sun would not have even set by that time in June. He paused at his front door, turning to wave goodbye just in time to see the craft shimmer and disappear from sight. The final shock of the day came when the clock in his kitchen said 11:53 PM.

Chapter 20: Dual Use

Jean-Luc stared at the empty wall across from his desk. A single nail protruded from the bare wall of his otherwise impeccably decorated office on the top floor of the Paris headquarters of Ashleigh Industries in La Défense. The nail was surrounded by a series of holes showing where the nail had been relocated several times while the position of the picture that had once hung there had been adjusted. The picture no longer concealed the damaged wall. The lithograph had been loaned to the Louvre for a special exhibition of lithographs from Jules Verne books, and Jean-Luc was waiting for it to be returned.

"Mr. Gilbert is here to see you, Mr. Gallatin," said the receptionist over the intercom.

"Send him in," said Jean-Luc.

Jean-Luc got up from his desk as Charles entered the office. "Charles, what a pleasure to see you. I tried to catch you at the Polaris Explorer launch reception, but by the time I was done with all the 'meet-and-greet', you had departed. I'm delighted that you accepted my invitation to meet in La Défense."

"Our paths seem to keep crossing," said Charles.

"Please, have a seat," said Jean-Luc, pointing to one of two opposing sofas. "Coffee?" he asked.

The bare wall punctured with holes and faded rectangle where the picture had hung caught Charles' eye.

“I really should hang another picture on that wall to cover those holes,” said Jean-Luc. “My original lithograph of Jules Verne’s *Albatross* from ‘Robur the Conqueror’ belongs there. It has served to quicken my imagination about the future of travel.”

“Lighter than air flight?” commented Charles. “I have a complete first edition of all of Jules Verne’s novels. I know this lithograph well. You say, you have the original lithograph?”

“Yes,” replied Jean-Luc. “I loaned it to the Louvre for a special exhibition. It was a bit tattered, and they are going to try to restore it. It should be back any day,”

Charles said, “Jules Verne was quite the visionary. It’s a shame that the *Albatross* is only fantasy.”

“Actually, that’s the reason I asked to meet with you.” Jean-Luc said, pouring coffee for himself and one for Charles into commemorative mugs from the Polaris Explorer launch. “Crème and sugar?”

“Just crème, *s’il vous plaît*” said Charles.

“Apparently, you have been dabbling in lighter than air flight, yourself,” said Jean-Luc. “I read about your failed venture in Aix-en-Provence, but I suspect there is more to the story.”

Charles paused to stir crème into his coffee, “We thought we had discovered some sort of antigravity technology proposed by the scientist that developed microfusion with me.”

“Cédric Rothschild?” queried Jean-Luc.

“Yes,” replied Charles, “but the idea has yet to gain any traction.”

“And the magic ‘pea’?” inquired Jean-Luc. “I know about your pitch to angel investors in Sofia. You showed a video of the ‘pea’ levitating.”

Charles took a sip of coffee and squirmed uncomfortably in his seat, trying to decide how to respond.

Jean-Luc continued, “My guys have studied your patent and inform me that there is no way your antigravity claims could ever be reduced to practice, but I don’t believe them. You are hiding something.”

Charles made no response.

Jean-Luc said, changing the subject, “You know, the Graf Zeppelins that flew in the mid-1900’s had a remarkable resemblance to Jules Verne’s *Albatross*. Lighter than air flight has been a dream from the dawn of civilization. We envy birds in flight. It is tantalizing to imagine being freed from the pull of gravity. Fantasy, is it?”

Charles still made no response.

Jean-Luc continued, “Your invention of microfusion has transformed commercial shipping—not only cruise ships but cargo ships, container ships, you name it. If there was a way to use microfusion to propel aircraft, ridiculously inexpensive global travel would become possible. I suppose you know about the portal technology being developed by one of our sister divisions. Travelling at five times the speed of sound in evacuated subterranean tunnels is interesting, to be sure, but being able to escape the earth’s gravity without being in orbit would change everything. There would be no more need for high-speed portals or container ships or aircraft as we know them. More coffee?" he said, holding up the thermos container.

Charles shook his head.

"There were rumors that the Germans had developed antigravity technology during the Second World War, you know. Every once in a while a credible claim emerges that it may be possible to build a device that defies gravity. Is it only just fantasy?" Jean-Luc asked, looking intently at Charles.

Charles replied, "There is a prevailing consensus within the government hierarchy that disruptive technology needs to be kept secret. The belief is that certain kinds of technology that might provide military advantages should not be made public. This was the case with microfusion, of course. People in the French Navy thought microfusion was such a huge force multiplier that they needed to keep it under wraps. For certain, microfusion provides a benefit for warships, but I argued vehemently to no avail that the benefits to commercial shipping outweighed the military advantage. This was not any different from the dual use of nuclear power used in submarines and ultimately deployed in container ships. I lost the argument and microfusion remained classified for way too long. It was a pleasure to attend the Polaris Explorer launch last week. I am looking forward to receiving royalty payments now."

"You are dodging the issue," said Jean-Luc. "Is there any merit to the claim of antigravity?"

Charles sat silently for a moment to collect his thoughts. Then he finally said, "I can neither confirm nor deny it. Any work, if it is going on, is highly classified."

"Ah," said Jean-Luc, crossing his legs and leaning back into the sofa. "So, there is antigravity work going on?"

"I have already said as much as I dare," said Charles.

"I can appreciate the need for secrecy," said Jean-Luc, "But the implications for antigravity on commercial travel are enormous. Ashleigh Industries only wants the inside track."

Charles stepped out of the Ashleigh La Défense headquarters building and was planning to head toward the metro station when it occurred to him that it was an exceptionally beautiful day. He decided to make the ten-kilometer trip to the Intelligence Ministry building on foot. His general state of health was up and down. He had good days and bad days, but this particular day was a good one. He loved Paris and would be able to savor every minute of the two-hour stroll which would take him across the Seine on the Pont de Neuilly, along Av. Charles de Gaulle, where he waved to all the pigeons, motionless or not. He passed the Arc de Triomphe, crossing the Seine a second time on the Pont de l'Alma into the charming neighborhoods of the 7th Arrondissement. He stepped into a used bookstore to see if they had a copy of 'Robur the Conqueror'—a book he had not read since childhood. He was only able to find a tattered, edited and abridged, 14th edition in English. The artist rendition of the original Jules Verne lithograph was pathetic, but for the price of 2 euros, it would suffice. He came upon a street-side restaurant where he decided to have lunch—a pint of draft beer and a single serving pizza at an outdoor table. He spent the next hour engrossed in the book before going on to the Ministry.

Stephan was just coming down the street when he arrived at the gate. The two greeted and went into the Ministry together.

"I had a somewhat awkward meeting with Jean-Luc Gallatin this morning," Charles said as they entered the elevator.

"Abraham is hoping that you will brief him about it," said Stephan.

"You were expecting me?" said Charles.

"Of course," replied Stephan.

Abraham was already sitting at the table in his office. "Come in, Charles," he said. "Tell me about your encounter with Mr. Gallatin."

"I think he knows something big is up," said Charles. "He wanted to discuss antigravity. I thought he asked to meet with me to discuss the royalty payments for microfusion."

"So, what did you tell him?" asked Abraham.

"Nothing," replied Charles.

Abraham turned aside to Stephan and said, "I think maybe it's time to read Jean-Luc into the program."

Stephan replied, "Perhaps. It worked in the case of microfusion."

"I suspect that he already knows more than he should," said Abraham. "If all he wants is an inside track, by bringing him into our secret project, he will be bound by his honor to maintain confidentiality. Jean-Luc is a trusted friend. I will take care of it."

Sensing that the matter was settled, Stephan started to get up from the table.

Charles said, "While I have your attention, could someone please explain to me how a supposed test flight lasting six minutes in the antigravity craft, turned out to be a return trip to my home—a distance of about 1100 kilometers? That works out to a speed of more than 3,000 meters per second. That's ten times the speed of sound! The sonic boom, alone, would have shattered windows all over France. And while you are at it, tell me why the time on my wristwatch was reading six hours behind the clock in my kitchen."

Abraham looked up at Stephan and said, "I will leave it to Stephan to explain it. I need to head out for another meeting."

"Come with me," Stephan said to Charles, heading towards the elevator. He punched in the code that took them to the basement. Then they walked out to the drone pilot breakroom, each selecting a coffee from the espresso machine and sitting at a quiet table in the back. Stephan asked, "The time has come for you to hear about the phenomenon of timecharging. The trip from Brittany to Cap-Ferrat really did take six hours. Our craft was lumbering along at a modest 200 kilometers per hour, but the perception of the passage of time inside the capsule was altered by the same phenomenon that produces antigravity. We call this difference between actual time and experienced time, 'timecharging'. The effect was discovered by accident during surveillance drone development. Originally, the electronic circuitry onboard the drones was enclosed in a plastic housing. To make the drones more robust, it was decided to enclose the circuitry inside an aluminum housing integral to the housing for the antigravity rotors. When they did this, the drones no longer responded to radio commands. The engineers assumed that the metal housing had compromised the performance of the antennas. In the process of determining the cause, however, one of the engineers observed that the onboard clock had been running slowly. The speed of the clock controlling the microcomputers that should have been operating at some ten gigahertz seemingly was running at only ten kilohertz—six orders of magnitude slower. The effect only showed up when the control electronics were placed inside an aluminum housing connected to the rotors. Once the antigravity rotors were spinning to produce lift, the time experienced by the onboard electronics slowed down with respect to time on the outside."

"If so," said Charles, "then it would be a simple matter to return to the plastic housings."

"That's exactly what they did with respect to surveillance drones," replied Stephan. "But during development of antigravity craft for carrying passengers, Pierre suggested that the phenomenon might be useful if the perception of the passage of time during flight were to be shortened."

Charles exclaimed, "Do you mean to tell me that even though the craft is travelling at ordinary speeds, passengers think they are travelling at hypersonic speed?"

"That's exactly correct," replied Stephan. "You experienced it. You thought we were up for only six minutes and felt that it was too short for a test flight."

"If the onboard electronics controlling the rotors are slowed down so much, how does the craft even work?" asked Charles.

"The microcomputers onboard don't know they are running slowly. We were having normal conversation and had no sense that anything was out of the ordinary. The only manifestation was the discontinuity in time between the interior and exterior that you experienced as the discrepancy between your watch and the clock in the kitchen." Stephan chuckled to himself. "So, Charles, this means you are now six hours younger than when we embarked."

"The implications for human travel are profound," said Charles.

"Yes," replied Stephan. "Think about it. A squad of special forces could be inserted into a hostile situation from a ship 1000 kilometers offshore, and they would arrive on scene totally refreshed and ready to go."

"And a little younger," replied Charles. "This explains the 'behind enemy lines' comment by Alexy. This is a lot to digest. I have many questions. I would think such a craft would be a sitting duck for surface to air missiles."

"Except that the craft is silent and invisible," replied Stephan.

"How about radar?" asked Charles.

"Even radar," replied Stephan. "As long as the outer shell is made with metal integral to the rotor housing, the craft is completely stealthy. A radar beam in the microwave frequency bounces back in the kilohertz range. No known air defense system would detect the craft."

Charles' brain was in overdrive trying to synthesize the implications of the timecharging phenomenon. "How do you control the craft from the ground, then, and how does the pilot communicate with ground control?" asked Charles.

"He obviously can't have a normal conversation," replied Stephan. "The microwave commlink at one gigahertz has a frequency of only one kilohertz onboard, which has a bandwidth that can only support a few primitive commands. There is a short antenna external to the craft for this," he said, "but it is barely visible."

"How does the pilot control the craft from the inside then?" asked Charles.

Stephan finished his coffee and stood up. "Once the rotors are switched on, the pilot doesn't have much to do until they are switched off again. I suspect that in the future there won't even be the need for a pilot."

Chapter 21: Extraction

"Nightclubs? Are you kidding? I was working twelve-hour days. When would I have had time for club-hopping," replied Alexy.

"Brothels?" asked the interrogator.

Alexy scowled, "No," he replied, "but now you have gone over the line."

"Listen, Dr. Sarkova," said the interrogator, "any irregularities in your lifestyle could place your life in danger. Let's discuss books. What books have you read in the past ten years?"

"You mean like *Das Kapital* or writings of Mao Tse-Tung?" Alexy shot back angrily.

"This is serious business," responded the interviewer. "Have you ever read subversive literature of any kind?"

"No," replied Alexy, "unless you consider Walter Isaacson's *Einstein* subversive?"

"Where do you get your news?" the interrogator asked, losing patience and trying to get back on track.

"I used to subscribe to *Le Monde*, but I canceled my hardcopy subscription a couple of years ago. Now I just monitor currents events online," replied Alexy.

"Did you ever write a letter to the editor?" asked the interrogator.

"No," replied Alexy.

"Make comments on a blog?"

"No."

The grilling went on for hour after hour for a solid week probing every detail of Alexy's life and habits.

"What do you say we pause for lunch?" said the interrogator. "There is a sandwich for you in the break room."

"Did you lace my Coke with sodium pentothal?" Alexy said, jokingly.

The frustrated interrogator went down the hall into his office where he found Stephan and Jacques waiting. "How is it going, Marc?" asked Stephan.

"Not very well," replied Marc. "I have interrogated a lot of people to determine if they are ready for undercover work. There is no way anyone would ever believe Alexy would sell out France to join a subversive entity like the Syndicate."

"We aren't expecting him to become a card-carrying Syndicate operative," said Stephan. "We only need him to infiltrate the Knights. All this requires is that he demonstrate a little sympathy with their cause."

"He doesn't have a dissident bone in his body," objected Marc. "And I don't think he could pull it off without a great deal of training as an actor. It would be too dangerous."

"You are good at this kind of thing, Marc," said Jacques.

"It would take months," replied Marc. "Alexy has a well-known public persona. You would have to sell the notion that he has been living a double existence. I have been probing for something we could exploit to create the impression that he has been living a lie."

Stephan said, "There's got to be something. We need him to get introduced to the Knights by his brother. I can imagine no better set up."

"It's just too dangerous. I can't authorize it," replied Marc.

"What if it was disclosed that he is a closet homosexual?" asked Jacques.

The office went quiet for a moment.

"I doubt that Alexy would go along. This would ruin him," said Marc.

Stephan jumped in. "With some training, I think he could pull this off. He has never had a serious girlfriend. His hatred for the Syndicate burns strongly and I think he would do almost anything to infiltrate them and deal them a blow for murdering his father."

"Perhaps he is in the closet already," Jacques suggested.

"Doubtful," said Marc. "This would have come out during my interrogation."

Stephan added, "We could have him fired from Neutronetics for embezzling. Then coming out of the closet would be the *fait accompli*."

"I never knew that you could be so cruel," said Jacques.

"In the spy business, it is the results that count. There is often a great deal of cruelty encountered along the way. Yes. It's dangerous. But that's what spies do."

"Still, it's cruel to ask Alexy to destroy his life for this," said Jacques.

"He doesn't have to agree to the plan," replied Stephan. "It's his choice. He is free to decline."

The three stared out into space as they contemplated what they were about to ask of Alexy.

"But I don't think he will decline," said Stephan. "Deep down, his passion to get even with the people who murdered his father drives him. This is the kind of passion that, once channeled away from simple vengeance, has the makings for a terrific spy."

"I have been given the thankless task of turning you into someone you're not," said Marc as he inserted his key into the lock on the front door of his villa along the River Marne east of Paris and east of the town of Meaux. "I spent my entire career training movie actors and actresses to take on the roles of the characters they portrayed in their films. Transforming you into a French dissident may be the greatest challenge I have ever faced."

Marc led the way into the dark foyer followed by Alexy. A grand divided staircase curved up to the floor above in classic grandeur. Switching on a few lights, he said, "Your bedroom is up those stairs on the right. The bathroom has just been remodeled, so I think you will find it comfortable. You will be here for at least a month so make yourself at home. I live here alone with my daughter. She should return home from work in about an hour."

Alexy picked up his valise and headed up the stairs. He fumbled in the dark for the light switch and inspected his new quarters. He was gripped by panic at the realization that he was on the verge of embarking on a mission that would forever alienate him from the comforts of the civilized world. He unpacked and went downstairs into the sitting room where Marc was positioned next to a gas fireplace catching up on his daily emails.

"There is a bottle of Cointreux on the table by the door," said Marc. "Help yourself. It will settle your nerves."

Alexy poured himself a shot glass and sat down across from Marc. He held up his shot glass to inspect the fine liqueur. "This is a lovely villa," he said.

"It has been in my family for six generations," replied Marc.

They heard the front door open. "Hello, Papa, I'm home," she said.

Alexy stood up and approached the foyer. The two stared at each other, having already been introduced by Stephan in the drone concourse at the Intelligence Ministry.

"I would like to introduce my daughter, Melissa," said Marc. Observing their mesmerized glaze he said, "But it seems that the two of you may have already met."

Alexy sat with Stephan on the park bench adjacent to the meeting hall in Marseille. "Zander will be here any minute. You should leave me."

"Marc thinks this is a very bad idea. It's not too late to back out," said Stephan.

"No," replied Alexy. "I want to do this."

The two sat quietly. Finally, Stephan reached into his shirt pocket and took out a pack of cigarettes and handed it to Alexy.

"No thanks, I don't smoke," he said.

"And that's a very good thing," said Stephan. "These are not for smoking. There is an emergency transponder embedded in the bottom of the pack that gets activated when you take out a cigarette. When you get into a desperate bind and need immediate extraction, take out a cigarette." He stood up and said, "Good luck," and walked away, passing by Zander unnoticed.

Alexy and Zander embraced in a way warmer than Alexy had ever experienced. Zander said, "I can't believe you accepted my invitation to come to the Knights of Equality meeting at their headquarters in Marseille. This is a major rally that I think you will find invigorating." Alexy made a slight wave to a motionless pigeon nearby as he followed Zander inside.

The meeting hall was filled with raucous zealots. Many had flags or banners on poles. There was chanting and outbursts among the thousand or so gathered. There was someone speaking from the podium, but no one was listening and the sound coming from the public address speakers was mostly the squeal of feedback from the underpowered system. No one noticed.

Then there was a great cheer as the main speaker walked to the podium and the crowd quieted down somewhat. "Don't you think the time has come to put the world's rich and powerful in their place?" he boomed. The crowd went wild, and bedlam broke out making it impossible for the speaker to continue.

"Isn't this exciting, Alexy?" Zander was jumping up and down. "It's happening. The world is finally going to be set free from tyranny!" he shouted.

From time to time the charismatic speaker would scream some inflammatory comment into the microphone and the crowd would go wild once again. By two in the morning, the crowd had thinned. Zander pulled Alexy aside and said, "Come with me. There is someone that wants to meet you." Alexy followed Zander backstage. With a proud smile he said, "Meet Comrade Zalmony, the leader of the Knights."

Alexy recognized him immediately as the main speaker and held out his hand. Zalmony pulled him in for an embrace. "Welcome to the Knights," he said. "We are having a reception for a few honored guests. Would you care to join us?"

They walked for some time through the dingy back alleys of Marseille. Had it not been for the contingent of well-armed bodyguards, Alexy would have feared for his life. They entered a building with soldiers in battle fatigues and assault weapons standing guard at the door. The reception was raging. Several people were laying on the floor or plopped in chairs passed out with empty wine bottles by the sides.

"It seems that they started the party without me," Zalmony said with a deep laugh. "Come, I have a room in the back." Alexy and Zander started to follow. One of the bodyguards stepped in front of Zander. "Just him," he said pointing to Alexy.

Alexy followed Zalmony, who instructed him sit on a sofa and nodded to the bodyguard to leave them and pull the door closed. Zalmony sat on the sofa next to Alexy and put his arm around him. He felt Alexy flinch. "You aren't really gay, are you?" he said standing back up. "No problem," he said handing Alexy a shot glass of cognac and sitting down in a chair across the room. "I'm not in the mood anyway. So, Alexy, what do you think of the Knights so far?"

Alexy took a sip of the liquor and faded into unconsciousness, before he realized he had been drugged.

He awoke several hours later with a pounding headache. Zander was sitting next to him. They were both zip-tied to chairs facing a large metal desk where Zalmony was seated. "Show some courtesy and give these poor fellows some coffee," he said to one of the bodyguards, who splashed a cup of scalding coffee into Zander's face. Zander started howling in pain.

"Alexy and Zander, Alex-Zander... it's ironic that both of you are named after your father," Zalmony sneered from his swivel chair behind the desk. "Now, Dr. Sarkova," he continued, "tell me about timecharging."

Alexy squirmed in his restraints without effect. "I don't know what you are talking about," replied Alexy. The bodyguard approached him with a second cup of scalding coffee.

"What do you want to know?" Alexy asked.

“Everything,” replied Zalmony.

“Tell him what he wants to know,” screamed Zander.

“I need a cigarette,” said Alexy.

“You don’t smoke,” said Zander.

“There’s a lot about me you don’t know,” Alexy replied. “Cigarette please. The pack is in my shirt pocket. Zalmony nodded to the bodyguard to retrieve the pack, removing one and placing it between Alexy’s lips. “Light please,” he said.

Zalmony waved a propane lighter in the air. “Tell me about timecharging,” he said.

Alexy was still groggy from the drugging and the pain in his temples was overwhelming. He closed his eyes and shook his head to try to dispel the cobwebs.

“You are stalling,” said Zalmony taunting him by waving the lighter. He reached in the top desk drawer and withdrew a handgun. He took off the safety and shot Zander in the head. “His whimpering was getting on my nerves,” he said, pulling back the slide and loading another round into the firing chamber. He pointed the gun at Alexy. “Tell me about timecharging,” he whispered slowly.

Alexy saw a bright red dot appear on Zalmony’s forehead, which turned black almost instantly, before a trail of blood began to trickle down his face. He slumped down in his chair still holding the loaded gun in his hand.

The stunned bodyguard turned around just in time to see the flash of the knife blade that severed his throat. Alexy spat out the cigarette as he was being freed from the zip-ties. "Bring my brother," he ordered one of commandos. He went behind the desk and swiveled Zalmony's chair around. He pulled a small black notebook from the coat pocket and put it inside his own shirt.

Alexy and the two commandos, one lugging Zander over his shoulder, slipped out of the window, scrambled down the alley and climbed the fire escape to the roof of a nearby building. One of the commandos had a lanyard around his neck which he pulled out from behind his body armor. He pressed a button and almost instantly a hemispherical craft appeared out of nowhere. Stephan was at the door as Alexy, and the commandos climbed in. Alexy plopped down in one of the jump seats next to Stephan, out of breath, his head still throbbing.

"I'm really sorry about your brother," said Stephan.

"We were never close," replied Alexy. "He was just a delusional idealist. He should have known he was dealing with ruthless people."

"You sure didn't last very long on the inside," said Stephan, "I think eighteen hours may be a new record for a rooky spy mission."

"They already knew everything. My cover was blown from the beginning," Alexy said. "They wanted to know about timecharging. How in the world did they even know that word?"

"We were totally unaware that Zalmony was such a high-ranking Syndicate figure. The mission was not a total failure, though," said Stephan. "You flushed him out. We just were not expecting this to unfold so quickly. It would have been nice, though, if you had been able to penetrate the operation more deeply to get more intelligence on the Knights."

Alexy pulled the black book out of his shirt and handed it to Stephan. "Perhaps this will help."

Stephan thumbed through the pages that contained coded names and contact information for numerous Syndicate operatives. There was a folded sheet of paper in the back of the book that Stephan took out and inspected. "Zalmony was such an idiot," he exclaimed. "He left the cypher key in the back of the book." Then looking over at Alexy with a broad smile, he said, "You just might make a terrific spy after all."

Chapter 22: Mugs

"I am so sorry about your brother," said Abraham, pouring himself a mug of coffee from the carafe on the credenza, before joining Alexy and Stephan at the table in his office.

"I need to go to Sofia to tell my mother. She will be heartbroken," said Alexy.

"That won't be possible," said Abraham. "You are being hunted down, and we cannot protect you there." He took a sip of coffee, adding, "Anyway, it was imperative that we fake your death."

"Yes," Stephan said. "It appears that Zander was killed in a bar fight in Marseille, and you died trying to defend him. Your mother will be receiving two urns of ashes shortly—one containing the ashes of Zander and the other containing ashes from my fireplace."

"What? She thinks I am dead?" asked Alexy looking intently at Stephan. "She will die from a broken heart!" he exclaimed.

"That's unlikely," said Abraham. "She has been told the truth, that you are alive and well."

"And my sister?" asked Alexy.

"Yes," replied Abraham. "Mariam knows you are alive. She and the boys have gone to Uganda to be with her husband. The Agency has arranged for your mother to be relocated to a retirement home in Paris where she will be safe and receive the care she requires. Once the threat to your life subsides, you will be able to visit her."

At that moment, Jacques briskly entered. "Sorry to be late," he said. "There was a fatal accident on the autoroute that backed up traffic for miles. It seems that the victim was an employee in the Navy's procurement division." He grabbed a mug from the credenza and turned it over. "Limoges. Very good choice," he said filling it with coffee and joining the others at the table.

All eyes were on him for an explanation. "It turns out that the woman killed in the accident was responsible for procurement of everything distributed to the Navy commissaries. One of the items she was supplying was coffee mugs like these," he said, holding his up. "It seems, she was not procuring ordinary coffee mugs. Hers had a very sophisticated eavesdropping device embedded into the porcelain. The microcircuitry is made from silicon carbide—very clever, I must admit. The device is activated by heat when filled with hot coffee and picks up conversations and transmits them on a low frequency band not generally used for bugs."

Abraham, Alexy and Stephan each lifted their mugs to check the manufacturers' mark. "I estimate that there are more than 10,000 of these commemorative mugs distributed around navy facilities and ships, not to mention all those distributed as gifts or stolen and taken home," said Jacques.

"You're not serious," said Stephan.

"As a heart attack," replied Jacques. "Sorry Charles! There haven't been just a few moles here and there, as we had suspected. There are thousands. It seems likely that every secret conversation has been monitored for years."

"This is a catastrophe," exclaimed Abraham. "These aren't just leaks. It is a dam burst."

"How about my interrogations in Toulon by Marc Demoins?" asked Alexy. "Is that how Zalmony knew everything?"

Jacques nodded affirmatively.

"I am exhausted," said Alexy. "And this news doesn't help. I need to go home to Villefranche to recover from my ordeal."

"That won't be possible," said Stephan. "Your landlord has been notified of your death."

"What?" exclaimed Alexy.

"We have arranged for a safe house near Versailles," said Stephan. "You will have around-the-clock protection until this blows over."

"And all the stuff in my apartment?" asked Alexy.

"We have arranged for storage," said Stephan.

Alexy drained his coffee and returned to the credenza for a refill. "This can't be happening to me!" he said.

Abraham pressed a button under the table, and shortly two agents appeared at the door. The bulges under their hoodies revealed their assault weapons. "These agents will see you safely to your new temporary quarters," Abraham said.

Alexy stood and followed them to the elevator. He was in a daze and did not say goodbye or hear the goodbyes of the others. One of the agents pressed the code sequence to descend to the basement. Alexy walked stoically between the agents across the concourse toward the door at the end.

"Wait a minute," he said. "There is something I need to do." He quietly stood behind one of the drone pilots and placed his hands on her shoulders. She swiveled in her chair, and jumped up, wrapping her arms around Alexy's neck. "The last time I saw you was outside the meeting hall in Marseille when you waved at the pigeon. I never thought I would see you again."

Melissa wiped the tears of unexpected elation from her eyes.

"I will contact you when I can. Dinner perhaps?" Alexy queried.

Melissa stood rejoicing as she watched Alexy and the two bodyguards disappear into the corridor leading to Gare Montparnasse.

Jacques stopped by Saint-Jean-Cap-Ferrat on his way back to Toulon to see Charles. Gabrielle greeted him at the door. "Charles is expecting you on the terrace. You are just in time for lunch. I was preparing some sandwiches. Will you join us?" she asked.

"That would be wonderful," Jacques said, heading out through the sliding door towards the pool. Charles was relaxing on a chaise lounge for the first really hot day of summer.

He stood up to greet Jacques. He was drinking iced tea from the commemorative mug from the Polaris Explorer launching. Jacques took the mug out of Charles' hand and dropped it on the flagstone.

"What in the world are you doing?" exclaimed Charles.

Jacques stooped down to gather up the broken pieces. He placed his index finger to his lips to have Charles be silent. Then he took the Swiss Army knife out of his pocket and snipped one of the protruding wires with the scissors. "There," he said. "It's okay to talk now." Charles looked on in bewilderment.

"These mugs have embedded listening devices." Jacques held up the piece with the protruding of wire he had snipped off. "This is a tungsten filament antenna," he said, peeling off the label of what had been attached to the bottom to reveal a recessed cavity where he pried out a tiny microchip using the knife blade. "Just as I suspected," he said with a grin, holding it up to Charles. "I think I owe you a new coffee mug, though."

Gabrielle walked out to the terrasse with a try of sandwiches. "What happened to your mug?" she asked looking down at the pile of porcelain chards.

"Jacques was just about to explain it," said Charles, going to the cooler to fetch two cans of beer. Handing one to Jacques, he said jokingly, "Do you suppose the beer cans are bugged?"

Jacques took the question seriously. "Not as far as we know," he said. "The transmitters are heat activated, so I wouldn't expect them to work inside a cold beer. Actually, now that I think about it, since you were drinking iced tea there was nothing to worry about with your mug."

The three sat around a patio table under an umbrella to escape the heat. Gabrielle distributed paper plates and passed the tray of sandwiches.

"The scheme was very clever," said Jacques. "Plain white ceramic mugs were being imported by a company in Morocco that does custom decoration. The imported mugs were being replaced with identical copies that have the tungsten antennas embedded in the wall of the ceramic. Then they applied a custom decal with the desired logo. After a low-temperature firing to melt the colored glass of the decal, a silicon carbide microchip is installed in the recessed cavity in the base. The cavity is potted with epoxy and a label is applied that looks just like the original."

"Why silicon carbide?" asked Charles.

"To make them microwave safe, I suppose," replied Jacques.

Charles whistled. "Everybody likes commemorative coffee mugs," he said. "I have a cabinet full of them."

"Yes, indeed," said Jacques. "You might consider having them X-rayed. Every naval vessel, every base, every contingent—you name it—gives them away at special events."

"How in the world did they pull this off?" asked Charles.

"It turns out that the Navy procurement clerk was receiving a generous kickback from the sale of every mug she was able to deliver," said Jacques.

"Syndicate?" asked Charles.

"Possibly," replied Jacques. "We can't tell. It was motivated by greed in any event."

"Was?" asked Gabrielle.

"She won't be doing it anymore," replied Jacques. "We took her out of business. Also, the pottery in Marrakech burned to the ground. Apparently, they were stacking pallets of cardboard too close to one of their furnaces. They don't suspect arson, but the incident is under investigation," he said with a wink.

"I guess there will be a lot of unhappy customers when their commemorative coffee mugs fail to show up in time," said Charles with a chuckle. He noticed a bird soaring overhead and grabbed his binoculars for a better look. "Just as I thought," he said with a grin. "I think it's one of yours."

"There are a couple of important matters we need to discuss," replied Jacques, reaching into his shirt pocket and handing Charles a check.

"Eight-hundred and twenty-five thousand euros!" Charles exclaimed.

Jacques replied, "You need to drop the criminal action against Alexy. He didn't embezzle a penny. It was all a setup."

"I don't understand," said Charles.

"It's complicated," replied Jacques. "There is also a more urgent matter, though. With the revelation of the coffee mug fiasco, the neutron winder is no longer safe here in Beaulieu. It needs to be moved to a more secure location."

Chapter 23: Heavy Lift

"Welcome, Charles," said Jean-Luc, rising from his desk at Ashleigh Industries in La Défense. "Come on in. I have been expecting you." He directed Charles to one of the opposing sofas in his office. "What can I do for you?"

Charles said, "Abraham told me I could talk to you about antigravity engines."

Jean-Luc got up from his seat and quietly closed the door. Sitting back down he said, "Coffee?" There was a silver serving tray on the coffee table between them with a carafe and two mugs. Each picked one up and instinctively inspected the bottom. "Limoges," commented Jean-Luc. "Do you have any idea what I had to go through to recall all the commemorative mugs I had distributed after the Polaris Explorer launch? Is it true that the factory in Marrakech where the mugs were produced burned down?" he said, expecting no reply.

"I see that the Louvre returned your Jules Verne lithograph," said Charles.

Jean-Luc turned to look at the wall behind him. "It is really too small for the wall, but I adore the print and never found another one to keep it company," he said. "The lithograph was made by Julius Hetzel, the illustrator and publisher of many of Jules Verne's novels. I think you recognize this lithograph of the *Albatros*s airship. Lighter than air travel was a key fascination for Verne as it is for me."

"Which brings me to the reason for my visit," said Charles.

"Ah, antigravity," said Jean-Luc. "The dream of dreamers for centuries."

"It's no longer just a dream," said Charles. "It's real. How much did Abraham tell you?"

"Not much," replied Jean-Luc. "Abraham told me you might be able to explain it."

"That would be a reach," replied Charles. "I only understand the basics. The theory is very advanced, but the fact that the effect is real is no longer in doubt. I have first-hand experience with the antigravity aircraft and even travelled across France at Mach 10 in one."

"Mach 10!" exclaimed Jean-Luc sitting forward in the sofa. "Now you have my attention."

"As I told you before, antigravity is the most significant invention since the wheel, but I was never able to convince anyone that it is anything other than fantasy. That is when I was approached by a guy at the Intelligence Ministry named Stephan."

"Yes, I know him," said Jean-Luc.

"There was some rumbling within the Ministry that perhaps the scientist, Cédric Rothschild, was not such a crackpot after all. They inserted one of their agents to work with him on the theory," said Charles.

"Dr. Magdalena Roberts, I believe," volunteered Jean-Luc.

"It's quite possible that you know more than you are letting on," said Charles.

"The Intelligence Ministry wasn't the only party interested in Mr. Rothschild's theories," said Jean-Luc. "After all, it was Cédric that discovered microfusion. Did you know that Cédric fell in love with Dr. Roberts? He took her horseback riding and tragically, she fell off her horse and broke her back—paralyzed from the waist down."

"I was unaware. That is very sad. It must have happened recently," said Charles.

"Only a couple of months ago," replied Jean-Luc. "Cédric was devastated and has lost all interest in antigravity ever since, other than his obsession to build her a levitating wheelchair. That leaves you, Charles, as my only access to the technology."

"You know the work was classified, and remains highly classified," said Charles.

"But this may be changing," said Jean-Luc. "The current regime seems more open to giving access to secret technology that has significant commercial impact."

"That is why I came to see you," said Charles. "Surveillance drones disguised as pigeons are interesting for spying, but not very useful in the public sector. Six-seater antigravity craft might be useful for urban transport but..."

"How about time travel—timecharging?" interrupted Jean-Luc.

"Wow," said Charles. "Abraham told me not to discuss that with you. I really came to propose something a little more down to earth."

"I'm listening," said Jean-Luc.

"Heavy lift," said Charles. "Neutronetics has advanced antigravity technology from lifting a few grams to one-thousand kilograms over the past couple of years. This is all interesting and useful, but we are missing out on one truly important application. I want to build an antigravity device for lifting a thousand tons."

Jean-Luc leaned back in his chair, stunned. "I can hardly imagine the implications. Is this possible?" he asked.

"Actually, yes," said Charles. "That is why I am here. I proposed the idea to Admiral Charboneau recently because it occurred to me; why put microfusion reactors on warships to make them faster when it might be possible to make them weightless? He is an old friend and didn't actually come out and say I had lost my mind, but it was clear from the way he said, "Let me think about it", that he wasn't interested in redirecting years of naval research away from microfusion propulsion."

"So, you are thinking of container ships, perhaps?" queried Jean-Luc.

"Did you ever play the game of *boules*?" asked Charles.

"Yes, but never very well," replied Jean-Luc.

"So, you can imagine holding one of the balls in your hand," said Charles. "A typical ball is about 75 millimeters in diameter and weighs about 750 grams. If you were to throw one of these balls with all your strength horizontally, it might go a few tens of meters before hitting the ground. If the ball were fired out of a cannon at 1000 meters per second, perhaps it might travel a kilometer or so. Here's the interesting thing: this cannon ball would travel a few millimeters farther than conventional Newtonian mechanics would predict. No one could possibly detect this. It turns out that a mass travelling at high-speed perpendicular to the earth's gravitation field develops lift. A ring of one hundred boules mounted to the periphery of a rotating disc spinning at a very high-speed parallel to the ground might weigh a few milligrams less. Again, probably no one would notice.

Now imagine a boule made from nothing but neutrons, the mass would be astronomical—essentially the mass of a neutron star. Two such balls approaching each other at high speed would repel each other like the north poles of two magnets. This is what Cédric and Magdalena observed from high-resolution space imagery at the GRL that led to Cédric's classified and yet to be published antigravity theories."

Charles reached into his pocket to retrieve his leather pouch of neodymium iron boride magnetic balls. "These belong to my son," he said. "They are useful for illustration because the magnetic balls behave similarly to neutrons. This amorphous clump represents what goes into your microfusion engines. Deuterium fusion takes place because the speed of light is some nine orders of magnitude slower inside the clusters. But the random clusters have no net magnetic field, making them useless for antigravity." He pulled out a single strand of balls from the cluster of about one meter in length and laid it out on the coffee table. Then he wound the strand into a helical coil having a length of about 10 centimeters. Handing it to Jean-Luc, he said, "This is a structured coil, like the structured neutrons produced in our neutron winder. This toroidal form produces a strong magnetic field along the central axis. When the ends of a long coil are joined to make a hoop and mounted to the outside edge of a horizontal rotor spinning at high speed, you get the antigravity effect."

"Is that all there is to it?" asked Jean-Luc, handing the coil back to Charles.

"More or less," replied Charles. "The effect with hoops made from these magnetic balls would be barely detectable, but the effect with coils of neutrons is profound."

"You can produce enough lift to make them seem weightless?" asked Jean-Luc.

"Yes," replied Charles. "This is how the antigravity drones work. The largest we have built can lift a payload of about one ton. This is sufficient to insert 5 commandos into a war zone, but I have a bolder vision in mind."

"Passenger travel around the world at ten times the speed of sound!" exclaimed Jean-Luc.

"Not exactly," replied Charles. "That involves timecharging, and only the perception of time. But that is a different matter, and I am not prepared to discuss it with you at this time. I am talking only about payload lift capacity. I envision a lighter-than-air ship, a dirigible like the *Albatross* if you like, with a lift capacity of one thousand tons. Such a craft would require one thousand rotors like the ones we are deploying now and would demand a huge industrial mobilization from a company like Ashleigh Industries."

"Ashleigh Airships!" exclaimed Jean-Luc, with an approving clap of his hands. "I like it."

"The neutron winder from Beaulieu is over here, Charles," said Pierre. "We used eight identical delivery trucks dispersed all over France to smuggle it here to the Plouzané facility to confuse any Syndicate spies. We did not relocate the proton generator, though. It is a commercial system, and the Syndicate can highjack it if they want. We are building a replacement with ten times the proton flux, in any event."

Charles asked, "What is the status of the new winder?"

"Follow me," he said, leading Charles and Jean-Luc Gallatin to an adjacent workshop. "It is coming along nicely. I think it will be complete at about the same time as your new facility west of Brest at Phare Du Portzic," he said to Jean-Luc.

"I sure hope it will work," said Jean-Luc looking directly at Charles. I have a lot of money going into this project and I would hate to have to tell the Board it's for naught."

"Oh, it will work, sir," said Pierre. "At least the neutron winding part. Scaling a manufacturable production craft is up to Ashleigh Airships."

Chapter 24: Skeletons in the Closet

Alexy stood on the platform at the Versailles metro station flanked by his security detail. His routine consisted of going into the Intelligence Ministry two or three times a week and going to his office on the second floor. His knowledge of the Moldavian language and customs was essential for unravelling the inner workings of the Knights of Equality coupled with the clues from the black book he had taken from Zalmony's coat pocket. He had known it would be there because the night before the assassination, he watched him take it out and write something in it before joining Alexy on the sofa. The black book turned out to be a treasure trove of information. The full extent of the Knight's influence had not previously been fully appreciated. It was discovered that the organization was not just a recruitment tool for the Syndicate, but the rallies were used as a cover event for meetings of senior Syndicate operatives. With the cypher, it was easy work to identify the names of several of key figures and where they could be found. By the time they realized the extent of their security breach, several of the top people had been eliminated in freak accidents that could not be readily explained. Alexy hated this unsavory aspect of the job, but at least no one at the IM had proposed that he do "wetwork" in the field.

The cypher key was now useless because the cypher code had been changed. Alexy's role was to listen to conversations recorded by surveillance drones during the previous hours to detect subtle linguistic irregularities in the conversations which signaled they were speaking in code. The computers did a good job of translation into English and French, but artificial intelligence was not sufficiently advanced to pick up the code nuances of the conversations. For example, "I think it's going to be a hot day," was code for "get out of town right away". Upon entering the IM from the Gare Montparnasse station, Alexy stopped by the desk of the dispatcher on the drone flight concourse who handed him a hard drive containing the gigabytes of recorded conversation and video from the previous day. He would be spending his day listening for code fragments that could be added to the secret Syndicate lexicon.

Melissa was at her station. Alexy wanted to go over to say "hi", but she was engrossed in operating her drone, so he decided it would be unwise to disturb her. He took the elevator to the second floor, filled his thermos with coffee from the commissary, went into his office, plugged the drive into his computer and put on headphones for what he was sure to be another uneventful day. He had learned to listen to conversations at twice normal speed.

He was about to doze off when he heard the words, "Fred Flintstone". He jumped out of his chair to rewind the segment. It was recorded by a drone from the city of Burgas on the western shore of the Black Sea. He knew the place because his mother had taken the family there on holiday. She had adopted his cousin, Frederick, after his mother died in an influenza epidemic and his father, Frederick Rosca, was away from home fighting in the civil war. Frederick was about the same age, and he and Alexy had become close. They called him Fred Junior, but he hatted that name, preferring to be called Fred Flintstone after his favorite cartoon character.

Alexy grabbed the hard drive and scrambled up the single flight of stairs to Stephan's office. "You have got to hear this!" he said plugging the drive into Stephan's computer and rewinding to the place with the correct time stamp.

"Fred Flintstone is on his way," said the one speaking into his mobile phone. "I am heading to the airport now to pick him up."

Stephan looked perplexed. "Fred Flintstone?"

Alexy repeated it again more emphatically. "My cousin, Frederick! Who else could it be."

"I don't understand," replied Stephan.

"It would not be unusual for Frederick to go to Burgas," said Alexy. "He has a villa there. What is unusual is the person making the call. He is a known Syndicate operative."

Stephan stood up and said, "Come with me."

Abraham was in his office talking to another agent. Stephan stood at the door to catch his attention. "Can we pick up later?" Abraham said to the agent he had been talking to.

Stephan and Alexy entered and took seats at the table. "You are going to want to hear this," said Stephan.

Alexy began to recount the story, "I grew up with my cousin, Frederick, in Sofia. Frederick's father, Frederick Rosca, was my mother's brother. He was killed in the Moldavian civil war. Fred Junior, as we called him, hated that name and, as stupid as it sounds, wanted to be called, Fred Flintstone as a child. He is now the Manager of Blackseas Holdings, one of the largest commercial investment banks in the world. He lives in a villa on the coast north of the city of Burgas. In nearly forty years no one would have used the name Fred Flintstone unless he has adopted it as his code name. This morning, I was doing a routine analysis of last night's chatter when I heard the name, Fred Flintstone. I nearly fell out of my chair. When I listened to it again, there was a known Syndicate operative on a mobile phone in Burgas that said he was heading to the airport to pick up Fred Flintstone!"

Abraham looked over at Stephan, "Will you leave us please."

Stephan walked out and pulled the door closed behind him.

"Something big is up," said Alexy. "You need to dispatch me to Burgas to check it out. What if my cousin is a Syndicate operative? Since everyone thinks I am dead, I have the perfect cover."

Abraham put up his right index finger. "Hear me out," he said, giving Alexy a moment to settle down. "There is something very important I need to tell you. It pertains to the letter I gave you from your father to your mother."

Alexy remained quiet while Abraham drained his third coffee of the morning.

“There’s a lot to the story that you don’t know. The time has come for me to relate it to you,” Abraham filled his mug with water from the decanter. “When the Moldavian dictatorship was toppled, the country was splintered into numerous cartels, each warring with one another to fill the power vacuum left over from thirty years of brutal dictatorship. Bands of freedom fighters were formed to combat the chaos and try to restore some order. I had just been discharged after fulfilling my military service. I was young and idealistic, but to be honest, I was just looking for adventure. I went to Moldavia where I was assigned to the unit of your father and uncle, Frederick Rosca. We fought together as freedom fighters and ended up forming a loyal bond. We were as close as brothers could possibly be.

In those days there was no Syndicate, per se, but various factions established regions of political influence. These cartels were fragile and easy to destroy. This was aided by the fact that, whenever a cartel leader rose to prominence, he was quickly eliminated in a drone strike. The cartels became leaderless in short order, and this was not conducive to taking over the country by force. They ultimately discovered that their common political objectives would be better served if they joined forces. The cartels morphed into what ultimately became the Syndicate—an amorphous entity with collective ambitions to take over Moldavia, but without the political hierarchy typical of a ruling junta. Power was shared and command and control was carried out covertly.

The approach worked, and this is when the civil war started going badly for us.

"One night we were on a covert mission to blow up a railroad bridge. Why freedom fighters were being tasked with blowing up a railroad bridge remains a mystery to me, but that was our assignment. In any event, we were caught in the act of placing explosives and taken captive. Your father and I were held in the same prison. We were told that your uncle was being held in a separate prison for interrogation. This made sense to us at the time because Frederick knew much more about our counterinsurgency than either of us did. One night, your father was dragged out of our cell into the courtyard and shot dead. I watched the whole thing through the bars of the cell window. I was sure I would be next and spent the next few minutes preparing to meet my Maker. Then I heard explosions and much yelling and automatic weapons fire. Several fellow counterinsurgents opened the prison door and whisked me away in a hail of gunfire. They arrived too late to save your father, but I owe them my life. Before your father was executed, he gave me the letter to your mother that you now have.

"After a couple of weeks, Frederick Rosca reappeared claiming that he had escaped from prison. I had been reassigned so I gave the letter to him to deliver to your mother. He never did. You have probably guessed by now that it was your uncle that betrayed us—your mother's brother! Shortly thereafter, he disappeared, and everyone assumed that he had been killed in the war.

"Several years later I was a young officer in the Intelligence Ministry doing covert field work. A person of interest named Thomas Sanguine—an obvious pseudo-name—came to our attention as a high-level Syndicate operative. He was a particularly ruthless individual having committed at least ten murders. Our Agency wanted to apprehend him and bring him to justice for war crimes. When the mission briefing packets were circulated, the photo of the target individual, Thomas Sanguine, caught my attention. It was the eyes. The eyes don't change with plastic surgery. I knew in my heart that it was Frederick Rosca. So, I volunteered for the mission, taking with me a new recruit named Stephan.

Abraham leaned forward in his chair and spoke resolutely, "What I am about to tell you is shocking and you must never relate it to anyone, including your mother and sister. Do you understand?"

"Yes, sir," replied Alexy.

"Do I have your solemn promise?" asked Abraham.

"Yes, sir," replied Alexy. By that time, the shock of hearing the story about his father and uncle was setting in and he had become frighted by Abraham's demeanor—a demeanor that he had never seen before in the mild-mannered director.

"Stephan and I were dispatched to Burgas to capture Thomas Sanguine, a.k.a. Frederick Rosca—your uncle—and bring him back to France. The moment I saw him I knew for sure that it was Frederick Rosca, the traitor that had betrayed me and your father. The look of terror in his eyes when he saw me confirmed that he recognized me, as well. Rage got the best of me. I was not authorized to bury three 9 mm rounds into his chest. Stephan is the only other person on this planet that knows what I did that night. We turned over Frederick's office looking for any useful intelligence information. The letter I gave you was taped to the bottom of the middle drawer of his desk."

Alexy's head was spinning. What Abraham had told him was a lot to take in. He finally asked, "What about my cousin, Fred Junior? How did he become a Syndicate operative?"

"I think you may have drawn the wrong conclusion," replied Abraham. "Just because he was being met at the Burgas airport by Syndicate operatives doesn't necessarily mean that Fred Junior is a Syndicate operative. It is possible that the Syndicate operative you heard were using the code name, Fred Flintstone, pejoratively. His father left him a sizeable fortune, a fortune obtained by extortion and corruption. It is likely that he has some of his father's debts to pay. Black Seas Holdings is known for money laundering. Fred Junior may simply be the victim of blackmail or an extortion scheme. Perhaps you should consider this?"

Abraham got up from the table and opened the door for Stephan to come back in, nodding to him that the work was done.

"So, Stephan," Abraham said. "Apparently Alexy thinks he is ready to go back out into the field. He also informs me that he doesn't care much for his new name. I agree that it is rather commonplace. There must be a million Alex Smiths in the world, but that's the point. It makes it a lot easier to fabricate his cover story."

"How about just 'Smithy'?" suggested Stephan with a chuckle.

Alexy made no response. He was too much in shock from what Abraham had just told him to worry about his name or health status. The idea of going back out into the field to pursue his cousin had suddenly lost its appeal.

He was in the habit of meeting Melissa at the end of her shift and accompanying her on the purple metro line. He would go with her all the way to the end of the line and see her safely to Villa Demoins before returning to the safe house in Versailles. After several months of this routine, they began stopping for dinner in Meaux on the way to her villa. This day, however, he sent her a text message that he would be returning home early by himself.

Chapter 25: New Start

Alexy and Melissa sat together holding hands across the table in the back of the quaint restaurant they frequented in Meaux. "I have never felt like this about anyone before," Alexy said. "These last few months have been the most wonderful of my entire life. I didn't know it was possible to be so in love."

Melissa smiled at him in a way that Alexy knew the feeling was mutual.

"Now that my security detail has been relieved, we finally have some privacy," he said. There was a long silence as the flicker of the candle on the table danced on their faces. The dinner menus were yet to be opened, and the server sensed that he needed to leave them alone.

"I resigned from the Intelligence Ministry today," Alexy said. "I am burned out and ready for a change. I thought I wanted to learn the business from Stephan and go back out into the field. But in reality, I don't think I have what it takes."

"What will you do, then?" asked Melissa.

"I don't know," he said. "I received an offer to teach physics at a prep school in America. I have decided to turn it down," he replied.

"Why?" she asked. "That would be perfect. It would give Alex Smith a new beginning."

"Melissa, I just can't stand the thought of being away from you," he said. "Anyway, I detest that name. Alex Smith! That's as bland as it gets."

"How about Alex Demoins?" Melissa asked.

"What?" said Alexy.

"Well, I sure can't become Melissa Sarkova," she said.

"Are you proposing marriage?" he asked.

"It's plain you never will," she replied.

"You want to marry me?" Alexy whispered, tears beginning to run down his face.

"Papa, Alexy has something to ask you," Melissa said to her father as he was heading into the kitchen. He leaned into the refrigerator to fetch a bottle of beer with his back to Alexy.

With as much composure as he could muster, Alexy said, "Mr. Demoins, sir. I would like your permission to marry your daughter."

There was a momentary pause before Marc turned around smiling and holding a bottle of champagne. "It's about time," he said.

Marc and Melissa Demoins stood together in a small anti-chamber near the back of the Cathédrale Saint-Étienne de Meaux. "You look absolutely stunning in your mother's wedding dress," he said. "It is a shame that she did not live to see you like this."

Melissa stood quietly by his side and said, "Papa, am I making a big mistake?"

"Do you love him?" he replied.

"Yes," she said.

"Then that's the only thing that matters," he said.

"But, Papa, aren't you worried about the age difference? I am thirty-three and Alexy is forty-seven."

"Then you better get busy if I am going to have a grandson to inherit the Demoins estate."

The organ began to play the processional, and an attendant entered the chamber announcing, "It's time." Marc held Melissa's hand as they walked past row after row of empty pews to the front, where the first pew on the left was occupied by Charles and Gabrielle Gilbert, Alexy's sister Mariam, her husband, and sons, Matthew, Marc, Luke and John, sitting between them. His mother, Elena was seated in her wheelchair on the isle. Jean-Luc Gallatin was seated on the right with Abraham, Stephan and Jacques Rousseau. Marc walked with Melissa up the steps to the nave where the priest was standing and handed her off to Alexy before taking his seat next to Abraham.

The liturgy of Holy Matrimony was a short and solemn affair, followed by the priest's proclamation, "I now pronounce you husband and wife." Alexy and Melissa turned around holding hands with joyful countenance on their faces. "I present to you Mr. and Mrs. Alexander Demoins," said the priest.

The small wedding party exited the cathedral and got into a waiting van that took them to the outskirts of Paris where they passed through a security gate and entered a hangar-like structure for the wedding reception. Although the entire wedding was carried out in total secrecy with security personal everywhere, it was, nevertheless, a joyous occasion. Cyril, the Intelligence Ministry chef, had prepared the wedding cake, which was on a table in the center of the hangar bay along with an assortment of snacks. Cyril and another server poured wine for the guests.

Off to the side was a large black hemispherical craft with "Ashleigh Airships" stenciled over the door. The cargo bay of the craft was filled with Melissa's and Alexy's belongings for their relocation to the secret research and development compound of Ashleigh Industries in Cabo San Lucas. The site was chosen as one of the few places on earth not compromised by Syndicate influence. When the United States annexed Baja California, they systematically eradicated all the cartels and disinfected the entire peninsula. Jean-Luc had asked Alexy and Melissa to join the team of scientists and engineers tasked with developing a global network of antigravity transportation capsules.

"I am rather envious of you two going off to a dream destination," said Abraham to the newlyweds.

Jacques joined in on the conversation, "It is a shame that we couldn't reliably protect you here in France. It seems that you made a lot of enemies by taking down the Knights of Equity, so now it seems we must send you off to paradise to keep you safe."

Stephan added, "Perhaps if you were to do something as notable, Jacques, you could be reassigned to Cabo." This jab brought on laughs.

Jean-Luc jumped in. "With hypersonic transport, we can all vacation in Cabo whenever we want."

"Assuming we won't be missed for the three days of timecharging," said Charles.

"I don't know what you are talking about," said Melissa.

"Didn't Alexy tell you?" said Jean-Luc. "We will arrive in Cabo in under an hour, but it will take the craft we are travelling in three days to catch up with us." This brought a chuckle to everyone except Melissa, who remained perplexed.

"Don't worry," said Abraham. "None of us understand timecharging either. Maybe Alexy can explain it to you."

As the party was winding down, Jean-Luc suggested that it was time to depart. "I will accompany you to Cabo, if you don't mind," he said. "I have arranged for you to have a lovely secluded oceanside bungalow, not far from the lab."

"Now I'm really jealous," said Stephan.

Marc was standing quietly to the side. Melissa went up to him, "Are you okay, Papa?"

"Just sad," he replied. "After your mother died, you became my whole life. Now my little girl is going away." His composure was lost and tears formed in his eyes.

Melissa hugged him affectionately. "You have Henri and Camille," she said. "They will take good care of you, and we will video chat every day."

Alexy hugged his mother and sister goodbye and gave his brother-in-law and nephews a formal handshake.

Marc looked over at Alexy, "Alexander Demoins," he said. "You took your father's first name and my surname. This makes me very proud. In two weeks of intensive interrogation, I was unable to uncover a single serious character flaw. I opposed sending you undercover on the Knights mission because I was afraid that no one would believe you could be so duplicitous. I was right, you know, but we will never know for sure since your cover was blown from the start. Anyway, I am proud to have you as my son-in-law. Melissa is a handful, as you know. Please keep her safe."

Alexy hugged Marc as the two had completely lost their composure.

Alexy and Melissa turned to blow kisses from the doorway of the craft and toss her bouquet. Jean-Luc and the pilot were already on board. The stairs were raised and door closed. The faint sound of the antigravity rotors was drowned out by the goodbyes and cheers of the wedding guests. The craft shimmered momentarily into translucence before becoming completely invisible. The hangar door was opened, and the craft disappeared with the only telltale being the ten-centimeter-long antennae dangling from the underside.

Abraham turned to Alexy's family, who were standing in amazement at the sudden disappearance of the craft. "Perhaps you should forget what you just witnessed."

Chapter 26: Timecharging

"So, Alexy, I want to hear about this thing they were talking about during the reception," said Mellisa.

"Me too," said Jean-Luc

"Timecharging?" replied Alexy.

"Yes," said Melissa.

"It's very complicated and I wouldn't be able to do it justice in the forty-five minutes remaining for our flight, but I will try to give an introduction," said Alexy, selecting an apple from the fruit basket on the seat next to him. "Everything seems perfectly normal, right? We don't feel weightless, our speech is normal, our hearts are pumping at eighty beats per minute..."

"Except mine," said Jean-Luc. "It's pounding at 120 beats per minute."

"That's the result of anxiety and high blood pressure, Jean-Luc," said Alexy, "not timecharging." He tossed the apple into the air and caught it with his other hand. "See? Perfectly normal. The apple behaves the way it would on earth because we are under the influence of the earth's gravitation. The downward force of gravity is 9.8 meters per second-squared times the mass of the apple. The apple has no sense, whatsoever, that our speed relative to the ground is some ten times the speed of sound any more than the apple on the surface of the earth is aware that the earth if travelling through the universe at some enormous velocity. If our craft were travelling at a speed approaching the speed of light, this would be different, but even at 10,000 meters per second, our speed is only a fraction of the speed of light. This is the principle of relativity. If we were in an ordinary aircraft, one might look out the window and observe we are passing over the ground below at the glacial speed of about 200 kilometers per hour. The 10,000-kilometer flight from Paris to the southern tip of the Baja Peninsula would take 50 hours, not including stopovers for refueling and stretching our legs. The trip in a supersonic transport would still require sitting in an uncomfortable seat for five hours, and the plane would need lavatories and food service." Alexy took a bite of the apple. "What you are experiencing now is a revolution that will forever change the way people travel."

"Thanks for the advertisement," said Jean-Luc. "I wish I had captured it on video."

"So, back to timecharging," Alexy continued. "For this, you will need to allow me to delve into a bit of physics. First of all, I must remind you that energy is conserved. It is always conserved. This truth is captured by the first law of thermodynamics. Simply stated—it means there is no such thing as a perpetual motion machine. Conservation of energy is inviolable. In science fiction there is usually some sort of time travel involved or travel at speeds faster than the speed of light. The idea is tantalizing, but totally impossible because it would violate energy conservation. Timecharging is not time travel. It only effects the perception of time. Our trip to Cabo will still take 50 hours. We just won't experience 49 hours of it.

"If I were to shine a laser beam across this capsule and you had the means to measure its speed, you would find that the photons in the beam were travelling at 300,000 kilometers per second, and it wouldn't matter what direction I pointed the laser. If this were not the case, then the universe could not exist as we know it. Now, if it were possible to observe my laser from the ground—and this would, of course, be an impossibility—the laser would appear to be travelling at Mach 10. Furthermore, a measurement of the speed of the light from the ground would show 300,000 km/s less about 3.5 km/s for our forward velocity. A ground tracking station would clock our craft at 200 km/h, however, that very clever ground observer would clock my laser as moving along at only 299,996.5 km/s. That difference in the speed of light is the basis of timecharging. The time is not lost, it is merely experienced aboard this craft in a reference frame with a different lightspeed."

"What makes the speed of light different on this craft, then?" asked Melissa.

Alexy twisted off the top of a bottle of Chardonnay from the minibar and filled a wine glass for Melissa, another for Jean-Luc, and one for himself. "This takes us into an interesting, and controversial area of theoretical particle physis," he said, taking a sip. "The scientist, Cédric Rothschild, hypothesized that the speed of light is variable, which requires that mass must also be variable if energy is to be conserved. This notion got him into hot water during his PhD research days at Candlebridge in Great

Britain. At the time, the university was flush with research grants to study the mysterious particle responsible for dark matter in the universe. Dark matter and dark energy were proposed to explain the apparent mass discrepancy that could not be attributed to ordinary matter based on star luminosity and conservation of angular momentum in galaxies. Cédric claimed that dark matter was an artifact of apparent mass—that it didn't actually exist at all. Needless to say, such heresy did not sit well with the 'guardians of orthodoxy' at the university, and they conspired to have him expelled. He never did receive his PhD nor the Nobel Prize he deserved. I had the honor of meeting with him privately on several occasions. He is a very down-to-earth guy—kind and generous and never condescending.

"What Cédric proposed was that energy is, indeed, conserved according to Albert Einstein's famous formula, $E = mc^2$. But he also proposed that only the product of mass and the speed of light squared needed to be constant. As long as this product is invariant, the 'm' and 'c' could vary in such a way that the product remains invariant. Until recently, it was believed that the speed of light, 'c', is a universal constant. In fact, this assumption was taken on faith and never challenged. Furthermore, there was no way to confirm it experimentally because measurement experiments always give the same value and the parameters that determine its velocity also change in such a way as to give the appearance that the speed of light is invariant. In order to measure it somewhere else, on a distant planet, for example, you would have to travel there along with all of your measurement equipment. But by the time you got there, the speed of light would be measured to have the same value as was obtained on earth.

"Now for the fun stuff," said Alexy. "What is mass, really? As long as the speed of light is constant, the mass of an object is determined by its energy. But what if the mass could change while the energy remains constant? This requires that the speed of light also must change accordingly. By the same token, if it were demonstrated that the speed of light was observed to change, this would necessarily involve a change in mass. This is the point at which I entered the picture. I spent much of my career measuring what I thought was the rest mass of a neutron. It was straightforward to measure the kinetic energy of a fast-moving neutron based on the subatomic particles that emerged after a collision with a stationary target nucleus. Then it was a simple matter to calculate the mass of the neutron based on Einstein's formula. That is, of course, assuming that the speed of light in Einstein's formula is invariant."

At that moment, the hatch opened, the stairs deployed, and the luscious fragrance of a tropical paradise permeated the cabin.

Jean-Luc said, "Welcome to the Ashleigh Research Center. We just call it the ARC."

Alexy followed Melissa down the stairs. "Well, Jean-Luc," he said. "Melissa and I are about to begin our honeymoon, so I guess we will have to pick up the neutron story at a later date."

Jean-Luc replied, "I have a short meeting with the director and then I will be heading right back to Paris. When you two lovebirds decide to reemerge into the real world, let me know and I will come back to throw you a proper party."

Two golf carts pulled up. "I will leave you now," Jean-Luc said, waiving as he hopped into the first cart and sped away.

Alexy handed his valise and Melissa's suitcase to the driver of the second cart. "We will put the rest of your belongings into storage for when you want to collect them," said the driver.

Melissa jumped into the cart, tapping the crown of her wristwatch. "The time is right, but the date function on my watch appears to be all messed up," she said.

"Your watch is fine," replied Alexy. "But there is an aspect of timecharging that I will need to explain—later perhaps."

The grounds of the ARC were astounding. Lush green lawns were flanked by flower beds and blooming trees. The pungent odor was intoxicating. It was warm and humid, but not hot. The entire sprawling compound, located on the southeast tip of the Baja Peninsula at Bahia Terranova, comprised 1,000 acres. It was enclosed by a chain link fence with surveillance cameras and security guards in civilian clothes on patrol. A collection of modern buildings dotted the compound surrounding a central administration building and a 4-story apartment building for employees and their families. The driver pointed to an adjoining country-club-style building with a spacious terrasse with umbrellas and a pool. "You will find the dining hall in there," he said.

"It's so green here," exclaimed Melissa. "I'm sure we are surrounded by barren desert."

The driver pointed in the direction of a knoll to the north. "The microfusion reactors and desalination plant are on the other side of that berm. It is amazing what can be done with virtually limitless electric power and a million gallons of fresh water a day," he said.

They proceeded along a shady gravel road through a dense grove of trees, coming out the other side to a breathtaking view of the Pacific Ocean. Alexy and Melissa were speechless. It was no 'bungalow' as Jean-Luc had described it. Their future residence was an exquisite cottage on a cliff overlooking a small, protected bay with a white sand beach accessible by a set of stairs extending down from the cottage.

The driver pulled up to the front of their new quarters. He pointed to a footpath heading into the woods. "The main complex is only about 500 meters down that way," he said. Alexy and Melissa were not listening as they bolted to the front door. "Of course, you can always request a pickup," he called out in vain. He placed their bags just outside the front door.

On the side table in the front hall was a bottle of champagne in an ice bucket and a tray of crystal flutes with a card that read, "Best wishes for a happy life together. – Jean-Luc Gallatin."

Alexy and Melissa skipped dinner that evening and breakfast the following morning, but over lunch in the commissary Melissa said, "You told me that you would explain why my watch shows a date three days later than when we departed Paris."

"That's the miracle of timecharging," he said with a grin. "No jetlag."

"I guess I don't understand," she said.

Alexy replied, "We left Paris at about 3 PM on Saturday and arrived here just an hour later—eight time zones away— without any jetlag," he repeated. "You felt like the trip lasted only an hour, but in fact, it took three days minus the time we gained going west through eight time zones. You are actually three days younger than you were yesterday."

"Three days?" said a puzzled Melissa.

"Don't worry," he said. "You won't miss them. Now Jean-Luc, on the other hand, given the frequency of the trips he has been making here, he could possibly live forever."

Melissa did not get the humor. "This is all a bit weird don't you think?"

"Okay," said Alexy. "Here's a question for you. How fast would you have to travel going 10,000 kilometers from east to west to arrive one hour after you departed?"

She replied, "Here in Cabo we are in the Mountain time zone. There's an eight-hour time difference, you said. So, we gained eight hours and loose an hour for the trip duration, that would require that we travelled the 10,000 kilometers in seven hours. The speed would be 10,000 divided by 7."

"Precisely," said Alexy. "That would be 1,430 kilometers per hour, Mach 1.2—supersonic, but feasible. Now, what time would it be in Paris when you landed in Cabo?"

"The trip would take seven hours, so, I suppose it would be 3 PM plus 7, or 10 PM," she said.

"That's right," said Alexy. "In Cabo it would be time for an afternoon siesta, but your body clock would say it's time for bed. That's jet lag, of course. Now, suppose you were in some sort of craft that could land in Cabo at 4 PM Paris time, just one hour after departing Paris, but you also wanted to arrive in Cabo at 4pm in the Mountain time zone? You do that by timecharging."

"You lost me," said Melissa.

"With timecharging the clocks inside the capsule run slower than the clocks on the outside," said Alexy, "because when it is 4 PM in Paris, it is only 9 in the morning in Cabo. You need a way to alter the perception of time so that the sensation of the passage of time is altered. You need to compress the perception of time so that a one-hour trip from Paris to Cabo seems like a one-hour trip from Paris to London, for instance. Then there's no jetlag and your body clock is in sync when you arrive. The ratio of the real travel time to the perceived time inside the capsule is the time compression. In our example, the ratio is 7 to 1—that is, if we made the trip at Mach 1.2."

"Now you are telling me a fairy tale," said Melissa.

“All it takes is a way to compress perceived time aboard the craft so a 7-hour flight at Mach 1.2 seems like a 1-hour flight at 10,000 kilometers per hour. Here’s how it works. I instructed the pilot to make the trip last one hour. I could just as well have asked him to make the trip last five minutes, but I thought an hour would provide a relaxing time to chat and unwind. I also wanted to arrive in Cabo at 4 PM Paris time but have the time in Cabo also be 4 PM. The Ashleigh Airship can’t actually go anywhere near Mach 1.2. It is not possible to arrive on the same calendar day, so it needs to roll over into the next day.”

“But you said the antigravity craft was only going 200 kilometers per hour,” said Melissa.

“That’s right,” replied Alexy, “Our speed was adjusted by the flight computers to arrive in increments of twenty-four hours, plus the trip duration and minus the time change. That means the craft could have travelled 10,000 kilometers divided by 15 hours, if one day was added. Then our ground speed would have been about 667 kilometers per hour—still faster than the airship can travel. So, if we added two full days to our trip, that would have made our groundspeed 303 kph for the trip. We could have made it at that speed, but it is at the limit of what the craft can safely do. Rather, I settled on three days, or 65 hours, allowing a more comfortable speed. The time compression ratio was 65 to 1 in that case. Anyway, what’s the rush. We still arrived one hour after we departed Paris and at 4 PM in Cabo—just three days later—that’s all.”

Melissa consulted her watch. "You mean, we left Paris on Saturday the 17th of April and arrived in Cabo San Lucas on Tuesday the 20th?"

"Amazing, isn't it?" replied Alexy. "I have some ideas how to make the craft fly at supersonic speeds. Can you imagine circumnavigating the globe—some 40,000 kilometers—and arriving back where you started fifteen minutes later? That would require a ground speed of 10,000 kph–Mach 8!"

"Why not just arrive fifteen minutes before you left?" asked Melissa.

"That would involve time travel," replied Alexy. "I don't think it's possible, but I wouldn't want to be the test pilot who attempts it. He just might end up in a parallel universe," he said in jest.

"Welcome to the ARC," said a man approaching their table at that moment. "Allow me to introduce myself. I am Director François Wallace. I trust you are finding your accommodations satisfactory."

"Quite so," said Melissa.

"A very nice surprise from what we were expecting," added Alexy, getting up for a proper greeting. "Will you join us?" he said pointing to an empty seat at the table.

"Only for an instant," said Dr. Wallace. "I don't want to impose on your honeymoon. I only wanted to meet you and extend an invitation for a tour of the complex when you are ready."

"We plan to be doing a little exploring on our own," said Alexy, "but a formal tour would nice. I am eager to meet my research team. Tomorrow, perhaps?"

"What's the rush?" Dr. Wallace said. "I think you and Mrs. Demoins should spend more time together before you dive into work."

"Please call me Melissa," she said.

"Then you may call me François," he returned. "I suggest that I arrange for a tour and formal introduction to your team next Monday, then. Have you been to your private beach yet?"

"We were planning to go there after lunch," said Melissa.

François got up from the table and said, "It is a very special place. I think you will enjoy it."

Chapter 27: The Briefing

Alexy stood with Director Wallace in amazement in front of the test stand in the lab. A hollow tube about 5 centimeters in diameter and 2 meters in length was strapped to the workbench. He turned to look at the entire team that had assembled for the demonstration. “Am I to believe that you have already constructed a propulsion engine?” Alexy asked.

Director Wallace replied, “It was risky research, and we carried it out off-budget. Let me have the chief engineer, Etienne Guillard, explain.”

Etienne stepped forward. “Most of the people that are working on this project came from Ashleigh Marine where they developed the propulsion system for the Polaris Explorer cruise ship. As you know, the microfusion reactors on that ship generate steam for making electricity to power the ship’s screws. I came from a secret program within the Navy developing a new type of waterjet propulsion. I met Mr. Charles Gilbert, whom I think you know, on a sea trial for a new class of ultra-fast frigates. Mr. Gilbert was concerned that I didn’t know how microfusion worked, so I accepted the challenge to figure it out. He and Mr. Gallatin dispatched me to this project with the consent of my superior officer, Captain Rousseau, who was also on the X-Frigate sea trial.

“As you are aware, the problem with antigravity craft is lack of speed. Helicopters have the same drawback. Antigravity generates lift, just like a helicopter or a hydrogen dirigible, but there still needs to be some form of propulsion for lateral movement. A dirigible uses an ordinary aircraft propeller for this. In the case of a helicopter, however, the rotor is tilted forward, which results in some falling back to earth. By this, some of the potential energy of the craft gained by rising in altitude is converted into kinetic energy for forward flight. The helicopter engine must do considerable work to maintain altitude, but this is how lateral motion is achieved. This is the same for an antigravity craft, except that when the pitch of the axis of the antigravity rotors deviates from the vertical, lift is decreased, and the rotor must spin faster to maintain the same altitude during level flight. This imposes limitations on craft speed.

"The purpose of the ARC is to develop a line of craft for executive travel for Ashleigh Aviation. Timecharging solves the problem of flight duration and jetlag but does not address the desire of busy people to get places faster. The tube on the workbench in front of you is an attempt to address this problem. Initially we thought we would be designing craft with jet engines. This would have been feasible but involves carrying a lot of fuel onboard which impacts range. We put our heads together and a most remarkable idea emerged.

"Instead of wrapping neutrons into antigravity hoops, why not make linear coils, like springs, and employ the high magnetic field along the central toroidal axis to accelerate protons. We already had a neutron winder and a high-flux proton source here in the lab. The design is so simple I am almost embarrassed to talk about it. We had the device you see on the bench in front of you built in a week."

Etienne turned around and said, "Let's fire it up."

A short pulse of protons was introduced into one end of the tube and a blinding flash was visible at the other.

Etienne said, "We estimate that the protons exiting the tube are travelling about ten thousand meters per second. That means that with a proton beam current of just ten milliamperes the thrust would be more than 50 kilowatts. We can only operate the engine for a few milliseconds at a time because otherwise we would melt everything in the lab downstream of the engine. Once we miniaturize the proton source, we will be able to operate the engine on a tank of liquid hydrogen for hours—outside, of course. I can imagine antigravity craft travelling at Mach 10, notwithstanding sonic booms and the impact on air traffic control. The downside is that the passengers will continue to suffer jetlag unless they return to the same place they started from the same day."

Alexy commented, "I suppose this will make short business trips more convenient."

Jean-Luc and other Ashleigh Systems executives from the corporate headquarters in La Défense showed up on the video screen for the conference call at the scheduled time. Alexy had assembled some of the research and development team in the conference room at the ARC in Bahia Terranova.

"Good morning. That is, I should say, good evening in Paris," said Alexy, "I am here with Director Wallace and senior members of the research team. I thought it might be a good time to bring you up to date on our progress."

"I'm glad to see you have been enjoying your time in paradise," said Jean-Luc. "I hope everyone is getting along. I hand-selected your team from the Polaris Explorer microfusion propulsion project. They are a temperamental bunch, but very capable," he said.

"We are getting along just fine, sir," replied Alexy. "They have been working diligently with very little understanding of antigravity, but some very innovative ideas have been emerging, nonetheless. I think their familiarity with marine propulsion has opened their eyes to some new possibilities for antigravity craft."

"Good to know that some of the experience they gained working on microfusion is applicable," said Jean-Luc. "I have not been able to get away to join you in Cabo, as I had hoped. You never finished the neutron story on the trip down, so I thought you could take a few moments to finish this story for the benefit of me and the people I assembled for this video call."

"How technical do you want me to get?" asked Alexy.

"Don't dumb it down," said Jean-Luc. "I will let you know if you venture too far over our heads."

"Okay," began Alexy. "As I recall, we were discussing neutron rest mass. If I had some tiny tweezers, I could pick up a neutron and weigh it on an electronic pan balance. It would weigh 1.67 times 10 to the minus 27 kilograms, and we would call this the rest mass. This is total nonsense on many fronts, not the least of which is that such tiny tweezers don't exist. But the bigger issue is that we describe the neutron on the balance pan as being 'at rest'. At rest? What a foolish notion. A neutron can never be at rest. The idea that a neutron can ever be at rest is a total fantasy. The neutron on my balance pan has measurable energy, which is described by Einstein's formula, $E=mc^2$. If the speed of light, *c*, happened to be a universal constant, which we are now confident that it is not, then the neutron mass would be defined if the energy is known. What Cédric Rothschild demonstrated is that the speed of light and mass are coupled and their product constrained by the conservation of energy.

"The idea that the speed of light is variable is still not universally accepted, but anyone trying to explain microfusion and antigravity with fixed light speed gets entangled in a web of more and more complex contortions like scientists experienced in the 16th Century trying to fit the motion of planets in geocentric orbits. However, once variable light speed is accepted, some remarkable things start to make sense—microfusion, for example. What's more significant is that the mass is a manifestation of gravity. We say the rest mass is such and such, but this is only the case if the speed of light is constant. The neutron on my pan balance is being tugged down by the force of gravity. If we were to place a mole of neutrons on the balance pan, they should weigh about one milligram, assuming they were all at rest. The trouble is that we know that the cluster of neutrons would weigh 10^{15} times more, or more than one ton. How can this be? The answer is that the neutrons are not actually at rest. They are moving around at high velocity in random directions. This is important because it brings us to the difference between random clusters, like those in a microfusion reactor, and the motion of neutrons in a structured orientation, like the coil loops in an antigravity rotor. If I pursue this any further, we will end up going into a rabbit hole. Suffice it to say that the neutrons, when structured, combine to have a net magnetic field vector.

"Here is where matters become a bit more complex, so stay with me. If I fire a beam of neutrons horizontally and perpendicular to the earth's gravitation field at high velocity, they interact with the gravitational field. The mathematics are complex and involve a double vector cross-product, but the net result is an imposed torque that causes the neutrons to deflect away from the direction of the gravitational force. In a nutshell, this is antigravity. The neutron coils in the rim of an antigravity rotor spinning in a plane perpendicular to the earth's gravitational field have a torque sufficient to generate lift.

"Okay," said Alexy. "That's the Cliff's Notes version."

"It can't possibly be that straightforward," said Jean-Luc.

Alexy replied, "The science of antigravity is really not all that complicated in principle. It's the practical engineering where things get complex. My team and I have been studying lift mechanics. It's not too different from how a helicopter works except an antigravity craft requires no further power once it reaches its desired altitude, unlike a helicopter which needs power just to stay aloft. I must admit that building a craft with a million-kilogram payload capacity, as Charles Gilbert proposed, will be far more challenging than I imagined. An idea we have been kicking around is that, rather than moving a large cargo payload slowly, why not transport smaller payloads more rapidly."

"Tell me more," said Jean Luc. The other people on his end of the video call also perked up.

"Well," replied Alexy, "A large container ship, even with microfusion propulsion, has a top speed of only about 30 kilometers per hour. Say it carries twenty thousand containers. An 8,000 km voyage can take several months. As long as the recipients for the cargo are not in a hurry, this poses no problem, but what if you could ship a single container at supersonic speed and deliver it to the destination port the same day. The implications for perishable items like fresh fruit are profound. A single antigravity transport could deliver a few hundred containers, round trip, in about the same time it would take the container ship to make the journey."

This comment caused a buzz among the people in La Défense. "Did I hear you say, 'supersonic'?" asked Jean-Luc.

"These guys see no fundamental reason why not," replied Alexy. "It all comes down to a fluid dynamics challenge. There are no airfoils that cause most of the drag with conventional aircraft."

There was a moment of animated discussion on Jean-Luc's end. After it died down, he said, "You do know Alexy, that a supersonic antigravity craft obviates the need for timecharging."

"Yes, sir," replied Alexy, "and we could add widows!"

"This would have no small impact on the direction our executive transport division is taking," Jean-Luc said.

"Yes, sir," replied Alexy.

There was an extended pause on the other end. Finally, Jean-Luc came back on and asked, "How long will it take to build the first prototype craft?"

"If you let us redirect some of our engineering resources, we should have it by the end of the year," replied Alexy.

"We need to discuss this more thoroughly," said Jean-Luc. "Give us some time to think about it. I will come visit you in Cabo next week with a team of executives to assess the possibilities."

The video conference ended and the monitor screens at both ends went blank. There was a moment of complete silence in the room on Alexy's end followed by a raucous cheer by his team.

Book III

Chapter 28: Bleak Night

François informed Alexy and Melissa at dinner that Jean-Luc and a group of Ashleigh executives were on their way and should arrive at ten the following morning.

"Melissa and I adore the beach cottage," said Alexy, "but now that we are beginning to interact socially with the members of my team, we are feeling rather isolated and were wondering if it would be possible to arrange for an apartment closer to the rest of the team members."

"Certainly," said François. "I will take care of it as soon as Jean-Luc departs tomorrow."

Alexy and Melissa were knocked out of bed by eight large explosions in succession. Alexy glanced at the clock on the dresser—3:23 AM. They dressed quickly by the emergency light and grabbed the flashlights from the wall next to the front door of their beachside cottage. The blasts had blown in all the west-facing windows and shattered glass was everywhere. They raced down the footpath toward the main compound. When they emerged from the woods, they couldn't believe their eyes. The entire complex had been leveled. The only light was coming from smoldering fires in the rubble which revealed the extent of the devastation. The administration building and commissary were completely flattened. The silhouettes of dazed people wandering around the grounds could be seen among the flames.

The first fire engines were beginning to arrive. Their floodlights illuminated the horrific scene. They hooked up fire hoses but there was hardly any water pressure. Alexy and Melissa ran towards the employee apartment building to find that the four floors had collapsed like a stack of pancakes. A few people were climbing out of the rubble. Melissa had had emergency room training in the past and she began organizing a make-shift triage for the injured as ambulances began arriving. Alexy looked over at the crater where the research laboratory had stood an hour earlier. He recognized Etienne, apparently uninjured but dazed and in shock. There was total chaos during the ensuing hours before daybreak, when a contingent of marines began flooding the compound grounds. There were sixteen dead and twenty-three wounded with ten still unaccounted for by 8 AM. Direct Wallace's home had been destroyed but his body had not been recovered by that time.

The craft transporting Jean-Luc and three Ashleigh executives arrived right on schedule. The landing zone had been moved because the ARC ground controllers had not been responding to incoming calls. This was a good thing since the regular landing pad was filled with emergency equipment. Alexy watched for the translucent shimmer and change to black of the craft. He ran to the spot in time to see Jean-Luc standing at the top of the stairs surveying the scene in complete shock. Because of timecharging he had had no prior knowledge of what had taken place.

"What happened here?" he demanded as Alexy approached the craft.

"No one knows," replied Alexy. "There were eight large explosions in the middle of the night."

Jean-Luc walked slowly down the stairs trying to comprehend the carnage in front of him. His shock was beginning to transform into rage. "Where is Director Wallace?" he asked angrily.

"Unaccounted for, sir," said Alexy.

One of the drone operators in the flight concourse in the basement of the Intelligence Ministry in Paris called his supervisor over to watch what was unfolding on his video monitor. Once the supervisor had seen enough, she hurriedly extracted the backup hard drive from the console and ran to the elevator. Emerging on the 4th floor, she found Abraham and Stephan chatting. Abraham immediately sensed the urgency and signaled for her to come in. The supervisor proceeded to plug the drive into the video console and pressed play.

"This is surveillance drone footage from a few minutes ago," she said. The blinding flash of explosions saturated the video screen to white. "This is the ARC facility in Cabo San Lucas. Completely destroyed!" She rewound the video by about five minutes. "We have been tracking a Syndicate submarine for several days on the Pacific side of the Baha Peninsula," she explained. "About five minutes ago, which was 3:20 AM

Mountain time in Cabo, the submarine surfaced and launched 8 ballistic missiles, as you can see here. The missiles impacted on the Ashleigh Research Complex three minutes later."

"Good grief!" exclaimed Abraham. "This is horrible. The Navy has been claiming for years that there is no credible threat from Syndicate submarines. This should convince them that the threat is real enough."

"There is something else you are going to want to see, sir." She rewound the video by about an hour. "We picked up a fishing boat in the vicinity of the sub. This would not have been unusual at this time of year since the tuna are running, but it surprised us when the boat stopped right over the location of the sub, which surfaced with just the sail protruding. You can see a line being tossed and the fishing boat being tethered to the sail. Then you can see someone climbing a ladder and entering the sub through a hatch at the top of the sail. The fishing boat departed, and we decided to track it to see where it came from. By the time we got back on station, the submarine was on the surface firing missiles."

"Come with me," demanded Stephan as the two scurried to the elevator and descended to the drone flight concourse. He walked over to the flight console monitoring the sub and asked the operator, "Where is the sub now?"

"I don't know, sir," said the operator. "As soon as the missiles were launched, it submerged and made a deep dive to avoid detection."

“You idiot!” yelled the man that had transferred from the fishing boat as he entered the bridge. “If you had only waited one more day, you would have taken out Sarkova and the entire top echelon of Ashleigh Industries.”

“The fishing boat wasn’t available tomorrow night,” snapped back the skipper. “Perhaps you would have preferred that we just leave you behind.”

Chapter 29: Redirection

Alexy was met by Etienne as he departed from the antigravity craft.

"Did Melissa return to France with you?" asked Etienne.

"No. She wanted to remain at the hospital in La Paz to help with the injured," replied Alexy.

"The memory haunts me," said Etienne darkly. "I have been having difficulty sleeping. It's good to see you. I'm glad you were able to come. There is someone I am eager to have you meet."

"Where is here?" asked Alexy.

"Here is nowhere," replied Etienne with a chuckle. "This is the Intelligence Ministry's version of a black hole. It is so secret it doesn't even exist."

"We are somewhere in France, I presume?" asked Alexy.

"Most assuredly," replied Etienne. "In Brittany not far from the coast. It's a wonderful part of France, but this facility doesn't exist."

The two entered the lab, depositing all their electronic devices into wire Faraday cages that were stored in a rack just inside the door prior to going through metal detectors. Alexy followed Etienne up a flight of stairs to the research laboratory.

"I would like to introduce you to our theoretical physicist, Dr. Samuel Stevenson-" said Etienne.

"*Enchanté*," said Alexy.

"Delighted to finally meet you, as well," said Sam.

"You speak perfect English with no accent," Alexy observed.

"That's because I'm American," replied Sam. "I emigrated to France after the Great War. I was at the GRL at the same time you were at the Val d'Isère Institute."

"So, you must have known Cédric Rothschild," said Alexy.

"Indeed," replied Sam. "But I was among the scientists at the lab that thought Cédric had a 'loose screw'."

"How did you end up here, then?" asked Alexy.

Sam replied, "When Cédric started spouting his nonsense about the possibility of antigravity, I got my hands on a copy of his manuscript about variable light speed, which sowed doubts about certain fundamental views I had held dear. Microfusion was real enough, but we all thought there had to be an alternative explanation than light slowing down in supermassive objects. We had dismissed the idea because it clearly violates conservation of energy."

"Please explain," said Alexy.

Sam said, "Simply, the experiments he claimed to have carried out, that demonstrated that light slowed down when going through a tube of uranium could not possibly be correct. If light were to slow down, there is no way to account for the loss in beam energy. With microfusion, we never had to worry about this because the energy of deuterium fusion completely masked the effect. Then rumors began to circulate that France was carrying out experiments with antigravity and something called, "timecharging". I started poking around and the next thing I knew, I got hired to work in this laboratory."

Alexy laughed, "Yes, those things do seem to impact career paths."

"There's something I want to show you," Sam said, motioning for Alexy to follow him over to an optical bench. "I was compelled to reconstruct Cédric's experiment using a miniature version of the neutron toroid like the ones Etienne's team are developing for their propulsion engine." He put on a pair of safety glasses and handed Alexy and Etienne some to do the same. Then he switched on a krypton fluoride laser. The neutron tube was clamped to the optical bench with the axis aligned with the laser. The color of the laser beam exiting the tube was dull red.

Sam looked at Alexy triumphantly. "The short wavelength of the incoming laser is in the deep ultraviolet, but the wavelength of the exiting beam is six times longer." Alexy knew immediately the implications. "The light changes color to a lower frequency! Cédric was right. He was only able to detect a small change in the time of flight of his laser beam, but with a neutron toroid, the effect is enormous," he exclaimed. "But how is this possible? Where did the energy go?"

Alexy replied, "I presume you are going to tell me."

"Let's go into the breakroom for coffee," said Sam. "You will want to be sitting down when I describe my theory."

They each got coffee from the expresso machine and sat at a round table in the breakroom.

Sam began to explain, “The phenomenon is being called ‘timecharging’. The analogy to purchasing on credit is not terrible as far as it goes. I buy a car on credit and agree to pay back the bank with interest over time. Where does the interest come from? I must create it in the future. In the same sense with timecharging, I borrow time in the present on credit to pay it back in the future. But this is where the analogy breaks down.”

“Cédric proposed that during galaxy formation from a black hole, the speed of light increases as the galaxy expands. This is, of course, a clear violation of conservation of energy, right? Perhaps not. A black hole has almost no entropy because the light is in a frozen state. We have no problem saying that the entropy of that expanding galaxy is increasing. So, why can’t the speed of light be increasing in just the same way? But this would require a modification of the 2nd Law of Thermodynamics. It would demand that, just like energy and enthalpy, energy and light speed are coupled in some way. In other words, energy can be stored in the increasing light-speed just like the potential energy of a black hole is stored in its small entropy.”

“This sounds a bit like science fiction to me,” said Etienne.

“Fascinating,” said Alexy. “This would certainly resolve much of the mystery of timecharging. Have you worked out the mathematics?”

“Most of it,” said Sam. “Unfortunately, since the work is top secret, I can’t publish it and bounce these ideas off scientific peers.”

"Anyway," said Alexy, "I'm not so sure you would be well served by being pulverized by the guardians of orthodoxy. If you are willing to share your calculations with me at some point, I would like to dig into this matter more deeply."

"We need to go," Etienne said to Alexy. "You will have plenty of opportunity to spend time with Sam, but I want to show you our new engine before we head to town for dinner with Jacques."

The engine lab on the lower level was a flurry of activity with people motivated by the urgency of deploying an antisubmarine capability quickly. Etienne and Alexy stood in front of the new propulsion engine.

"We have made a lot of modifications since the ARC," said Etienne. "Fortunately, this lab already had a neutron winder after the one in our lab in Baja was destroyed, so we really did not lose all that much momentum."

Alexy walked around the test bench where the prototype engine was running continuously. A bank of monitors on the wall displayed several operating parameters, the most important of which, was the thrust indicator. Alexy studied it carefully. Turning to Etienne, he asked, "150 kilowatts? Is that correct?"

"Yes," replied Etienne.

"I don't see the proton source," Alexy said.

"That's what I was eager to show you," replied Etienne. "It turns out we don't need ions after all. At the ARC we assumed that it was the axial magnetic field that accelerated the charged protons, but this turned out not the be the case. We can thank Sam for this. He proposed that air would work just as well, so we hooked up compressed air to the front end and *voilà*—thrust! Sam explained that any gas molecules, ionized or not, will experience the timecharging phenomenon once inside the neutron tube. The magnetic field has nothing to do with it except to hold the neutrons together. He explained that, because the speed of light on the inside of the tube is some six orders of magnitude slower than on the outside, the molecules creep along at a speed so slow they are barely moving until they reach the end, where they shoot out at high velocity. How is this possible? I haven't a clue. Sam thinks it is like a coiled spring, where the enormous energy is stored in the lower light-speed somehow and released again at the exit. It's all a mystery to me, but the proof is on the workbench, in any event."

Alexy and Etienne entered the *Centre de Chiropratique Portzic* adjacent to the naval base at Brest. The receptionist said without looking up, "The office is closed."

"Please tell the captain that Dr. Alexy Demoins and Mr. Etienne Guillard are here to see him."

The receptionist looked up and said, "Oh, yes. He is expecting you. Go on back."

Jacques was waiting in the SCIF. He closed the door after they entered and engaged the locks.

"Welcome," said Jacques. "There are some things that I wanted to discuss in secret before we go to dinner. I know that both of you are aware that I am a captain in the French Navy and simultaneously working for the Intelligence Ministry. The recent missile strike on the ARC has precipitated a rather delicate matter. Vice Admiral Charboneau has consistently downplayed the threat from Syndicate submarines and now the Navy has been left unprepared. He sees the fleet of ultra-fast frigates as his legacy. These ships are designed for surface actions in the littorals but have only limited ASW capability as you both know. Repurposing these ships with active sonars, anti-submarine rockets and torpedoes presents a formidable challenge, and would be a stopgap measure, at best. Ultimately an entirely new class of warship will be needed, which would require years before they could be deployed. Furthermore, the Air Force abandoned the ASW mission years ago.

"Abraham has determined that even if the Navy were to go full steam ahead with such an endeavor, their heart is not really in it. I am about to reveal something very secret that must not leave this room. We have suspected for some time that there is at least one highly placed person in the Naval Directorate that has been working behind the scenes for years to keep the Navy from recognizing the emerging submarine threat and thwart any initiative to rectify the deficiency. I can tell you in truth that Abraham has been trying to sound the alarm for years, to no avail. This all came to a head with the Baja incident. He has taken it upon himself to expropriate the antisubmarine mission into the IM—not with warships, obviously, as this would be an afront to the Navy, or with aircraft, as this would be an affront to the Air Force—but with the antigravity technology that has come out of surveillance drone development. He believes that even very fast surface vessels are entirely too slow to meet the challenge. Even our new Nautilus class submarines are being sent to sea without torpedoes. The Syndicate has apparently deployed an unknow number of Soviet era submarines that have been repurposed with microfusion reactor propulsion which makes them stealthy and able to stay submerged almost indefinitely.

"I am about to tell you something that neither of you know. We—the IM, that is, not the Navy—were tracking the ballistic missile submarine that fired on the ARC. Had we had the means, we could easily have sunk the vessel as soon as the missile hatches were opened."

"You said you were tracking the sub," asked Etienne. "How did you do that?"

"Again, this information is top, top secret," said Jacques, "because we don't think the Syndicate knows their subs are being tracked or how we are doing it. Microfusion gives off copious quantities of helium gas that bubbles to the surface. If the subs are operating close enough to the surface, it is a simple matter to detect the helium before it disperses into the atmosphere."

"Of course," exclaimed Alexy. "That's genius."

“I am only telling you this because you both need to have a clear understanding of the mission for the craft you are designing. You already knew the urgency. Now you know the purpose,” said Jacques, rising from the table. “Now it’s time for the very best dinner cuisine that Brest has to offer.”

“Did anyone ever confirm that Director Wallace perished in the attack?” asked Alexy.

Jacques sat back down. “Okay,” he said. “Here is some more highly classified information that cannot leave this room. The submarine that was being surveilled by our drone had a rendezvous with a fishing boat prior to the launch to pick up someone. The drone tracked the fishing boat back to the marina where it had departed before returning to the location of the sub just in time to see it on the surface with the eight missile hatches opened.”

“Director Wallace!” shouted Alexy slamming his palms on the table. “I never did like the man.”

“Yes,” said Jacques. “We confirmed it the following day in interviews with the fishing boat captain.”

“Now we can go to dinner,” said Jacques.

Chapter 30: Extortion

Jean-Luc passed the letter across his desk to Abraham.

Baja was just a warning. St-Nazaire shipyard is next. Wire 100 million euros to the account number that will be provided to you at 2 am Paris time next Saturday. The account will stay open for only 10 minutes.

"Who in the world has the ability to open up a bank account, receive a wire transfer, and then close it ten minutes later?" asked Jean-Luc.

"How did you come by this ransom note?" asked Abraham.

"A guy handed it to me this morning as I was walking into the office," Jean-Luc replied.

"What do you plan to do?" asked Abraham

"Pay it, of course," replied Jean-Luc in a rage. "Ashleigh's aviation division in Baja is a heap of rubble. That was a six-billion-euro investment down the drain. Charles Gilbert's freight division is operating on fumes, and Ashleigh is on the brink of bankruptcy. If we were to lose the shipyard, we would be finished."

"At least now we know why the Syndicate attacked the ARC," said Abraham.

"Some consolation," shot back Jean-Luc. "Can you imagine the leverage for extortion the Syndicate now has? Where the heck is our Navy?"

Pierre had assembled all the department heads in the conference room at the Brittany R&D facility. "I want to apologize for what I am sure seems like lack of clear direction over the past few weeks, but our mission has been changing rapidly. A year ago, our focus was on small autonomous surveillance drones, then it switched to building larger craft to transport people. Now, our mission has taken an entirely new direction; antisubmarine warfare. The only common thread connecting the three is designing and building antigravity craft, where we have amassed considerable expertise." Pierre signaled to display his first slide, which showed ASW in bold print surrounded by flashing banners that said, "Top Secret".

Pierre continued, "Next slide, please. The three critical elements for the mission are SRL; stealth, rapid response, and lethality. We will be adding some elements to the mission profile that we have never dealt with before. For one thing, the craft will need to be amphibious. That is, it will be necessary to land the craft on water and deploy hydrophones. The old method of detecting helium in the atmosphere is ineffective when the submarine is submerged lower than about 100 meters. We need to be able to listen for the characteristic sound of helium bubbles collapsing under pressure. There is no need to develop this capability. Captain Jacques Rousseau is working on arranging for the technology to be transferred from the underseas research facility in Toulon. But we will need to miniaturize and adapt the sensors to deploy on an amphibious drone."

"Next slide, please." An engineering depiction of the proposed craft appeared on the screen. "The surveillance mission will be carried out by unmanned craft in much the same way we are familiar with using surveillance drones. The only new feature of these craft is that they will have the ability to land and takeoff from water. I have assembled a new team to tackle this challenge."

"Next slide, please." An engineering rendition with a larger craft appeared on the screen that caused a stir among the attendees. "That's right," said Pierre. "You all recognize this as the six-seater craft we have been building for the past year. There's a new wrinkle, though. This craft will be modified to carry laser guided munitions. We decided it would be best to separate the surveillance mission from the attack mission. We debated long and hard whether to carry out this mission in manned or unmanned craft. In the end, we concluded that the decision to deploy ordinance and send some fifty sailors to their deaths needed to be a human decision."

"Next slide, please." The slide caption read 'stealth'. Pierre paused momentarily as the slide video played showing an actual craft on the flight deck of a navy frigate, transforming through the intermediate translucent stage and disappearing into thin air. "You have all witnessed this many times, but you have never seen one of our craft taking off from a naval warship. And you still haven't. The video was staged. The Navy has no idea that we plan to deploy antigravity craft from their ships, and it needs to stay that way."

"Up until now we thought of timecharging as a convenience for the passengers. No doubt, that's the case, but what we have in reality is a cloaking device. Many of you probably recall the cloaking devices on Romulan warbirds in the Star Trek series popular in the last century. You remember that they had to decloak to fire their weapons. It's the same for us. Being invisible while timecharging is very nice for getting around undetected, but it is necessary to come out of timecharging to carry out the combat mission. In the past, this required landing the craft and spinning down the antigravity rotors. Alexy's team is working on how to turn timecharging on and off while in flight. This will be essential for making our mission possible."

"Next slide." The caption at the bottom said, 'Lethality'. "I'm sure many of you are struggling with this aspect of the mission package, as am I. But it is no longer sufficient just to track enemy submarines. As we all learned from the Baja incident, Syndicate submarines constitute an existential threat, and we must develop the capability to sink them. Since we have no ordinance capability at this lab, again, Capt. Rousseau will be handling the necessary coordination with the Navy, in secret, of course. He has studied the problem and believes it will not be necessary to deploy heavy torpedoes. He thinks all that will be required is to drop a small laser-guided explosive into one of the missile silos when the hatches are opened."

“Next slide, please. This brings us to the last challenge; speed,” Pierre continued. “Rapid response is key. It is not enough to detect and track a submarine. It will be necessary to position the attack craft over the target in minutes if we are to sink the sub before it is able to fire its missiles. For this, Etienne and his team have developed an ingenious engine that should be able to propel an antigravity craft at supersonic speed. This will make it possible to be on target anywhere in the world from properly positioned frigates in the few minutes required for an enemy sub to surface and prepare to launch its missiles.”

“Now, are there any questions?” Pierre signaled to turn off the video.

“Were you able to track the wire transfer?” asked Jean-Luc.

“Only as far as Bucharest,” replied Abraham, “Then it vanished. This is a very sophisticated bunch of criminals with an ability to manipulate the global banking system.”

Jean-Luc laced his fingers behind his head and put his elbows on the desk with a sigh. “This is such a disaster. You realize that the Syndicate will be able to extort money from companies like Ashleigh with impunity.”

“Not for long, my friend,” said Abraham. “Not for long.”

Abraham looked intently at Jean-Luc. “How did it come about that you hired François Wallace as director of the ARC?” Abraham demanded.

“Did they recover his body yet?” asked Jean-Luc.

"No," replied Abraham. "He wasn't killed in the attack. He was already safely aboard the ballistic missile submarine that destroyed the ARC."

All the color drained from Jean-Luc's face.

"Tell me how you came to hire him." Abraham demanded.

"He came highly recommended," said Jean-Luc. "He was running the Undersea Warfare Research and Development Directorate. Vice Admiral Charboneau personally recommended him."

"Did you know that François Wallace was not his real name? That he wasn't even French?" Abraham asked with increasing anger.

Jean-Luc was rendered speechless.

"Did it ever occur to you that he was a high-level Syndicate operative?"

"His credentials were impeccable," replied Jean-Luc weakly.

"Yes, impeccable," repeated Abraham, "and forged. His entire naval dossier was fabricated. How can something like this happen?" Abraham demanded with growing rage, getting up and storming out of Jean-Luc's office.

Chapter 31: Justice

Stephan and two others stood in the shadows of a side street in Odessa on the Black Sea. Each checked the status of their firearms and screwed on the silencers. A fourth member of his team was sitting on a bench across the street feeding a motionless pigeon. When François Wallace emerged from the restaurant with his bodyguards, the signal was given. Stephan and one other stepped out onto the sidewalk. Displaying practiced precision, there were several barely audible pops. Almost immediately Stephan and his team boarded the waiting craft around the corner. The antigravity rotors began to spin up and the craft shimmered and then vanished.

Marc Demoins was at the breakfast table before sunrise catching up on the previous day's news, as was his custom. Alexy came into the kitchen an hour later, prepared a mug of coffee, and joined him at the table.

"I think Melissa will be sleeping in," he said. "She is still quite shaken by the death of her friend. Everyone expected Carmella to recover but she finally succumbed to her injuries from the blast."

"Are all the others back in France?" Marc inquired.

"Yes," replied Alexy, savoring his first cup of many for the day. "Carmella was the last patient to remain at the hospital in

La Paz. She was too badly injured to transport, so Melissa stayed behind to be with her to the end."

Marc handed Alexy his tablet displaying the top news stories from the previous day. "Did you see this?" he asked.

Alexy read the headline,

"Dr. François Wallace, former head of research and development for undersea warfare in Toulon was murdered last night in a failed robbery attempt while vacationing on the Black Sea."

"I interrogated that man, you know," said Marc gloomily. "Something was just not right, but I couldn't put my finger on it. I am very good at what I do. There are always tell-tale signs when someone is lying, but that guy was so practiced that he believed what he was saying to be the truth. The best film actors are like that. They become completely invested in the characters they portray. If not, the audience can always tell they are pretending. I recommended against him for the job, but they overruled me and promoted him anyway."

Melissa wandered into the kitchen a bit groggy. "I thought you were going to sleep in," said Marc.

She poured a mug of coffee and joined them at the table. "The sleeping pills aren't working anymore," she said. "I just can't get the memory out of my head. I was holding Carmella's hand when she passed away. She was so at peace. She said she was looking forward to being with Jesus." Melissa broke down weeping and Alexy took her hand. She got up from the table leaving behind her untouched mug of coffee. "I think I will go back to bed," she said.

"She's a wreck," said Marc. "I'm glad you could come. She really needs you."

"There's not much more I can do on the project in Brittany," said Alexy. "The amphibious drones and manned flight prototype are done. So, the timing for coming here is good. The trauma of the sudden attack and seeing so many dead and dying has left Melissa very depressed. She received some solace in caring for the injured, but when Carmella died, she snapped."

"What is next for you then?" asked Marc.

"Melissa will be needing some professional therapy, I suspect," replied Alexy. "Once she is on the mend, I will return to Brittany for the test flights. I have succeeded in redirecting my emotions from the night of the attack into buried anger. All I want to do now is eradicate the Syndicate from the face of the earth."

"That is a worthy pursuit," said Marc. "But if you do it with the intention of extracting vengeance, you will be disappointed. Justice and vengeance are not the same thing. You may think that sinking Syndicate submarines will be fulfilling, but it never works that way. The Syndicate seeks to steal, kill and destroy. Justice demands that they be defeated, but you will never defeat them by trying to get even."

Alexy sat quietly sipping his coffee. "I have requested to be deployed on the first search and destroy missions," he finally said.

"Do you think that's wise?" asked Marc.

“The craft is still a prototype,” replied Alexy. “There is a lot that can go wrong.”

“Perhaps,” replied Marc, “but a combat mission? You are a scientist, not a soldier.”

“This is why you opposed sending me undercover on the Knights of Equity mission, isn’t it?” said Alexy.

Marc sat quietly without responding.

“The mission profile requires the ability to enter and exit the timecharging state,” Alexy said to break the silence. “We have been trying for a long time to switch off timecharging while in flight. The first time we attempted it with crash dummies, they got emulsified. What a mess! There is an American theoretician at the lab that explained that it was like catastrophic decompression in jet aircraft at high altitude where people get sucked out of windows. He explained that during timecharging, energy is stored by the reduced speed of light and that it needs to be released gradually. This is what takes place when the craft lands and the antigravity rotors slowly wind down. It just never occurred to any of us that the process was a part of light-speed ‘decompression’. During flight, coupling and decoupling the cabin from the rotor housing is not a matter of simply throwing a switch. That leads to emulsified crash dummies. It requires simulating what takes place when the rotors slow down. Obviously, you can’t stop the rotors in flight, or the craft will plumet to the ground.”

“So, how do you do it?” asked Marc.

Alexy flashed a satisfied grin and replied, “That’s classified, and I cannot tell you.”

Chapter 32: Requiem

Friction between the Navy Department and the Intelligence Ministry was growing by the hour. The Admiralty believed the antisubmarine warfare mission rightfully belonged to them. Abraham would have been glad to let the Navy take it over, but endless delays were precipitated by turf battles and squabbles about how the work should be carried out. In the meantime, seventeen ballistic missile strikes had been executed by the Syndicate subs on strategic, high-value targets with more than a 100 billion euros in losses and still there was no credible response except to pay the ransom demands. No one knew how much money had been paid out in ransom, because the extorted companies were reluctant to release the information to the public, but estimates were in the trillions. In a matter of months, the Syndicate was draining the financial resources of the entire world economy.

The Navy had refused to permit the Intelligence Ministry to deploy its antigravity ASW craft on frigates, which necessitated repurposing some unarmed cargo transports for the task. The bigger issue was that the Navy was dragging its feet to approve the sharing of any technology involving explosive ordinance. Without weapons, the IM deployed craft to the site of a surfaced submarine on several occasions and watched helplessly as the Syndicate fired missiles unchallenged.

Stephan backed the delivery truck up to the dock door at the Brittany R&D facility where Pierre and Etienne were eagerly waiting. They rolled up the rear flap of the truck to reveal stacks of green wooden crates.

"I only brought the warheads," said Stephan. "You won't need the rockets. Just strap one of these to a suicide drone and make a hard landing on top of one of the exposed missiles in a lunch silo."

"Where did you get these?" asked Pierre as forklifts were dispatched to remove the pallets and take them inside.

"I know people," said Stephan. "The warheads were left behind by the Americans when they fled Afghanistan. They have been sitting in a warehouse for sixty years. I hope they still work.

"Hellfire! You must be kidding," exclaimed Etienne.

"There should be 280 of them," said Stephan. "The Resistance had no use for the missiles because they had no aircraft, but they discovered that the warheads make terrific car bombs."

"How do you propose that we test them?" asked Etienne.

"Do you know of an ordinance bombing range nearby that we can access?" asked Stephan with his characteristic irony.

"I can tell that you have already figured this out," said Etienne.

Stephan replied with a mischievous grin, "Perhaps we could strap one to a drone and fly it far enough out to sea that when you set it off no one will notice. If car bombers know how to do this, surely you guys could figure it out."

Melissa started going back into work where she found reconnecting with old friends to be therapeutic. With the addition of amphibious drones to the piloting tasks, the Agency was woefully understaffed. Melissa was assigned to the amphibious section, where thousands of drones were deployed by that time. It had quickly become obvious that once a drone had landed on the water and deployed its hydrophones, a pilot was no longer needed until it was necessary to relocate the drone to a new position. The drones were outfitted with a remote sensor to detect the sound of collapsing helium bubbles. When a likely signal was detected, it was communicated to nearby drones. In practically no time, drone swarms began surrounding Syndicate submarines autonomously without any direct interference from the drone control room in Paris. This work resulted in Melissa's promotion to superintendent of the amphibious drone division.

After weeks of tracking submarines in this way, some patterns in the way the subs were being deployed began to emerge, the most significant of which was that after a missile strike, the subs tended to head towards a point along a major shipping lane at which point the sound of collapsing helium bubbles would cease. After a period of time, the signal would be reacquired as the sub moved away from another point along the shipping lane.

Melissa was studying the tracks of this strange behavior, which were assumed to be due to switching off the microfusion reactors for some reason. One day she noticed that the track was lost when the sub passed under a liquid natural gas transport ship. The mystery was solved when it was realized the ship was not transporting LNG at all but was disguised to look like an ordinary transport. The ship was actually hollow. The subs were surfacing into a cavity in the interior from below for replenishing. Most importantly, this solved the mystery of how the subs were rearming without ever being observed to go into port. This intelligence breakthrough was kept secret at the highest possible level until the IM was able to demonstrate the ability beyond just tracking submarines, to destroy them. In the meantime, tracking the LNG tankers provided a wealth of information regarding Syndicate operations with respect to port operations and strategy. The port of origin was Newark, New Jersey and the destination port was Odessa on the Black Sea. It was thought that the Syndicate submarine base was near Odessa, but no one ever detected subs passing into the Mediterranean from the Black Sea through the Bosporus. With Melissa's discovery, they realized that the subs were coming and going inside the fake LNG tankers. The biggest revelation of all was that the carnage inflicted by the Syndicate extortion operation was being carried out by only four ballistic missile submarines. The Syndicate apparently had no clue that their entire submarine operation had been uncovered. Abraham was emphatic that no aspect of this intelligence was to fall into the hands of anyone in the Navy. The responsivity for identifying moles within the Navy fell to Jacques. Remedial action in the event of a breach was left to Stephan's group.

Everything was in place. A ransom demand was received at a large semiconductor manufacturer near Glasgow. It was agreed that the ransom would not be paid, but France would be liable for damages in the event that the plant was destroyed. The IM tracked one of the Syndicate subs to a position 200 kilometers off the west coast of Scotland, where it came to full stop. A manned ASW attack craft was immediately dispatched from the Brittany R&D facility, arriving on scene in time to see the sub come to the surface. The craft hovered silently and invisibly above the sub waiting for the missile hatches to open. The weapons officer on board the antigravity craft was authorized to fire when ready. A suicide drone was dispatched with an armed Hellfire warhead attached. Once the missile hatches were opened, the drone was steered into one of the central missile silos and detonated. The resulting explosion was followed by seven successive explosions and an enormous fireball. The sub broke in half and sank to the sea floor with a series of creaks and groans that anyone listening to the sonar would never be able to forget.

A second extortion attempt was being carried out simultaneously off the coast of Portugal. An ASW craft was dispatched with the same catastrophic result. The following day, a third Syndicate submarine was detected trying to hide out in the Gulf of Riga by the Latvian Navy. After several attempts to get it to surface and a warning depth charge, the sub finally surfaced and surrendered. The fourth sub ran aground on the west coast of Africa, where the crew abandoned the boat and disappeared into the surrounding villages. The LNG transport was seized by the Turkish Navy while passing through the Bosporus. In just three days the Intelligence Ministry completely eliminated the Syndicate submarine threat. All the credit was attributed to the French Navy in the press releases that had been prepared in advance.

Chapter 33: The Mole

Charles and Gabrielle Gilbert were seated at the table in one of the more fashionable restaurants in Paris when Vice Admiral Adam Charboneau and his wife, Sonia, arrived. Charles and Gabrielle both got up from the table to greet their friends with warm embraces.

"We finally succeeded in finding time to get together for dinner," said Charles. "Gabrielle and I haven't seen Sonia for months. We have a lot of catching up to do. I ordered a bottle champagne to celebrate your stunning victory over the Syndicate."

"Forgive me for spoiling the occasion," said Adam, "but I came to tell you that I am stepping down from the Navy."

"What? That can't be!" exclaimed Charles. "This is your finest hour."

Admiral Charboneau said, "Charles, we have been friends since the Academy, and I have always cherished our relationship. There is no easy way to tell you this, but I am under investigation."

"This must be some kind of a joke," said Charles. "Come sit down. We can discuss this over dinner."

"I won't be staying," said Adam. "I am in no mood to dine. I just came to say farewell."

"No, no," exclaimed Charles. "You can't just walk away like that. What's going on?"

"I'm sorry," Adam said. "I need to go to the Admiralty to clear out my office."

"You must tell me," Charles demanded. "What is going on?"

Adam closed his eyes and bowed his head. "I got mixed up with some very bad people. That's all I can say. I will leave Sonia to have dinner with you, but I really must go. If you don't mind, will you see her home?" He turned and walked away without saying goodbye.

Gabrielle wrapped her arms around Sonia as she broke down weeping. "Adam has not been himself for the past several weeks," she said through sobs. "He wouldn't tell me what was wrong."

Charles quickly paid for the unopened bottle of champagne and the three walked out of the restaurant together.

Stephan was standing in the hallway at the Admiralty when he heard the single gunshot. He saw someone emerge from Admiral Charboneau's office and disappear down the staircase into the darkness. He rushed to the office to see Adam Charboneau slumped in his chair still holding his antique service revolver. Blood was no longer flowing from his right temple. Stephan checked for a pulse and felt none. Then went in search of the assailant.

Charles barged into Stephan's office the following morning yelling, "Did you assassinate my friend, Adam?"

"No," replied Stephan, not looking up.

"I knew him extremely well. He would never have committed suicide," said Charles.

"It wasn't suicide," said Stephan glibly.

"Then who shot him and made it look like suicide?" demanded Charles.

"It wasn't me and it wasn't suicide. That's all I can say," replied Stephan.

Epilogue

Marc was sitting in the dark at the breakfast table in his villa on the Marne east of Meaux. It was pouring rain. Alexy entered the kitchen and switched on the light, not expecting to see Marc sitting there.

"They identified the mole," Marc said gloomily.

"I heard," said Alexy. "That's good news, isn't it? So, why so glum?"

"It's just hard when someone you have known and respected for years turns out to be a traitor," Marc replied.

"Can I pour you some coffee?" Alexy asked. "I have some news that might cheer you up. You will be pleased to know that I accepted the teaching position in the Physics Department at the Sorbonne," Alexy said as Melissa entered the kitchen.

"That is good news," said Marc, perking up somewhat.

Alexy said, "You once told me that I was a scientist and not a soldier. I decided to heed your sage advice. Justice is better than revenge. An academic career probably won't provide nearly enough excitement for me given what I have been through this past couple of years, but the Syndicate will be back one day, and then, who knows?" he added. "In the meantime, Melissa and I have some news that should really brighten your day." Alexy wrapped his arm around Melissa's waist. They looked at each other with adoring smiles and Melissa said, "Papa, you are going to have a grandson."

www.ingramcontent.com/pod-product-compliance
Lightning Source LLC
LaVergne TN
LVHW050614100826
845148LV00011B/1590